A CHRISTMAS BEGINNING

A CHRISTMAS BEGINNING

Anne Perry

headline

First published in Great Britain in 2007 by
HEADLINE PUBLISHING GROUP

1

Cataloguing in Publication Data is available from the British Library

ISBN 978 0 7553 3430 8

Typeset in Times by Palimpsest Book Production Limited, Grangemouth,
Stirlingshire

Printed and bound in Great Britain by
Mackays of Chatham plc, Chatham, Kent

Headline's policy is to use papers that are natural, renewable and recyclable
products and made from wood grown in sustainable forests.
The logging and manufacturing processes are expected to conform to the
environmental regulations of the country of origin.

HEADLINE PUBLISHING GROUP
An Hachette Livre UK Company
338 Euston Road
London NW1 3BH

www.headline.co.uk
www.hodderheadline.com

To all those who have impossible dreams

So this was the Isle of Anglesey. Runcorn stood on the rugged headland and stared across the narrow water of the Menai Strait towards the mountains of Snowdonia and mainland Wales, and he wondered why on earth he had chosen to come here, alone in December. The air was hard, ice-edged and laden with the salt of the sea. He was a Londoner, used to the rattle of hansom cabs on the cobbles, the gaslamps gleaming in the afternoon dusk. The streets were always busy with the singsong voices of costermongers, the cries of news vendors, drivers of every kind of vehicle – from broughams to drays – and the air carried the smell of smoke and manure.

Here must be the loneliest place in Britain, all bare hills and hard, bright water, and silence except for the moan of the wind in the grass. The black skeleton of the Menai Bridge had a certain grace, but it was the elegance of power, not like the low, familiar arches across the Thames. The few lights flickering on in the town of Beaumaris behind him indicated nothing like the vast city he was used to, teeming with the passions, the sorrow, and the dreams of millions.

Of course, the reason he was here was simple: he had nowhere else in particular to be. He lived alone. He knew many people, but they were colleagues rather than friends. He had earned his promotions until he was now, at fifty, a senior superintendent in the Metropolitan Police. But he was not a gentleman, and he would never be that. He had not the polish, the confidence, the ease of speech and grace of movement that comes with not having to care what people thought of you.

He smiled to himself as the wind stung his face. Monk, his colleague of years ago, once even his friend, had not been born a gentleman either, but somehow he had always managed to seem to be one. That used to hurt, but it did not any more. He knew that Monk was human too, and vulnerable. He could make mistakes. And perhaps Runcorn himself was wiser.

The last case in which they had worked together had been difficult and, in the end, ugly. Now Runcorn was tired of the city and he was due several weeks of leave. Why not take it somewhere as different as possible? He would refresh his mind away from the familiar and predictable, take long walks in the open, think deeply, for a change.

The sun was sinking in the south-west, shedding brilliant, burning light over the water. The land was dark as the colour faded and the headlands jutted purple and black out of the sea, only the uplands ribbed pale like crumpled velvet.

How long was winter twilight here? Would he soon find himself lost, unable to see the way back to his lodgings? It was bitterly cold already. His feet were numb from standing. He turned and started to walk towards the east and the darkening sky. What was there to think about? He was good at his job, patient, possibly a little pedestrian. He never had flashes of brilliant intuition, but he got there. He had succeeded far more than any of the other young men who had started when he had. In fact he had surprised himself.

But was he happy?

That was a stupid question, as if happiness were something you could own, and have it for always. He was happy at times, as for example when a case was closed and he knew he had done it well, found a difficult truth and left no doubts to haunt him afterwards, no savage and half-answered questions.

He was happy when he sat down by the fire at the end of a long day, and took the weight off his feet, ate something really good, like a thick-crusted ham and egg pie, or hot sausages with mashed potato. He liked good music, even classical music sometimes, although he would not admit it, in case people laughed at him. And he liked dogs. A good dog always made him smile. Was that enough?

He could only just see the road at his feet now. He thought about the huge bridge behind him, spanning the whole surge and power of the sea. What about the man who built that? Had he been happy? He had certainly created something to marvel at, and change the lives of people far into the future.

Runcorn had untangled a few problems, but had he ever built anything, or did he always use other people's bridges as he travelled – where? No more than home to bed in an unfamiliar lodging house. It was comfortable, he would sleep well, he usually did. Certainly it was warm enough, and Mrs Owen was an agreeable woman, generous in nature.

The next morning was sharp and cold, but a pale sun struggled over the horizon, milky soft through a fine veil of cloud, which Mrs Owen assured him would burn off soon. The frost was only a dusting of white here and there, enough to make the hollows stand out on the long uneven lawn down to the big yew tree.

Runcorn ate a hearty breakfast, talked with her for a little while because it was only civil to appear interested as she told him about some of the local places and customs. Afterwards he set out to walk again.

This time he went uphill, climbing steadily until nearly midday, when he turned and gazed up at a sky naked of clouds, and a sea shimmering unbroken into the distance.

He stood there for some time, lost in the enormity of it, then gradually descended. He was on the outskirts of Beaumaris again when he turned a corner in the road and came face to face with a tall, slender man of unusual elegance, even in his heavy, winter coat and hat. He was in his mid-thirties, handsome, clean-shaven. They both stopped, staring at each other. The man blinked, uncertain except knowing that Runcorn's face was familiar.

Runcorn knew him instantly, as if it had been only a week ago they had met. But it was longer than that, much longer. The case had been one of suicide suspected to be a murder. John Barclay had lived in a house backing on to the mews where the body had been found. It was not Barclay whom Runcorn remembered with affection, but his widowed sister, Melisande Ewart. Even standing here in the middle of this bright, windy road, Runcorn could see her face as clearly as if it were she who were here now, not her arrogant, unhelpful brother.

'Excuse me,' Barclay said tensely, stepping around Runcorn as if they had been strangers, and walking on up the road, lengthening his stride as he went. But Runcorn had seen the recognition in his face, and the distaste.

Was Melisande here too? If she were, he might see her. Even a glimpse. Did she look the same? Was the curve of her hair as soft, the way she smiled, and the sadness in her that had haunted him ever since?

It was ridiculous for him to think of her still. If she remembered him at all, it would be as a policeman determined to do his job regardless of fear or favour, but with possibly a modicum of kindness. It was her courage, her defiance of Barclay in identifying the corpse and taking the witness stand that had closed the case. Runcorn had always wondered how much that had cost her afterwards in Barclay's displeasure. There had been nothing he could do to help her.

He began walking again, round the bend in the road and past the first house of the village. Was she staying here also? He quickened his step without realising it. The sun was bright, the frost nothing more than sparkling drops in the grass.

How could he find out if she was here, without being absurd? He could hardly ask, as if they were social acquaintances. He was a policeman who had investigated a death. It would be pointless to see her, and ridiculously painful. He was a fool even to think of it, and he despised himself.

He hurried on towards his lodgings, the safety of Mrs Owen's dining-room table and the cheerful conversation of strangers.

But he did not stop thinking of Melisande. The weather grew a little milder, well above freezing. He saw more than a hundred birds pecking over a field, and the farmer told him they were redwings. There was plenty of yellow gorse in bloom, and the occasional hellebore in gardens. He walked in the sun and the wind, once or twice in the rain, and over a couple more days learned his way about the shore to east and west of Beaumaris. He found favourite places, hollows out of the wind, the first sign of snowdrops that caught his breath with sudden pleasure, intimate rock pools where strange shells and seaweeds grew.

On Sunday he dressed in the one decent suit he had brought

with him and went to the morning service at the church nearest to the place in the road where he had encountered John Barclay. It was a solid stone building with stained-glass windows and a bell that rang out in the gusty air, the rich sound carrying across the town and into the fields beyond.

Runcorn knew why he was here, driven as if by the pull of a magnet. It had nothing to do with the worship of God, even though he entered through the great carved wooden doors with head bowed, hat in his hand and a mixture of reverence and hope making his heart beat faster.

It was hushed inside, an old church with stone floor and high ceiling crossed with great carved hammer beams. The light was hazy. Colours in the great windows showed the stations of the cross, and what looked like a woman following after the figure of Christ in the street. She kneeled to touch his robe, and Runcorn remembered a story of healing. He could not recall anything more except that there was something beautiful just beyond his reach.

The congregation was already seated and he slipped into a pew towards the side. He watched with interest, bowing his head as Barclay passed by him, then lifting it again with a sudden pang of disappointment that Melisande was not with him. But there was no reason for her to be on this wind-scoured island in its barren glory, its wild coast, its birds, and the roaring sea. What was there here for a beautiful woman to do?

Then another, entirely different woman, perhaps in her

mid-twenties, walked past the end of his pew and on up the aisle. She moved with a unique grace, almost fluid, as if she were not touching the hard stone of a church floor with her boots, but were barefoot on grass, or the smooth sand of a beach. Her head was high, and when she turned, her pale face quickened by a secret laughter, as if she understood something no one else did. She was wearing dark green, so sombre it appeared almost black, and her cloud of hair escaped the rather rakish hat she seemed to have put on at the last moment, without thought. Her eyes were peat brown, and wide. Runcorn knew that, even though she looked at him for only an instant.

She went on up to the very front row, and sat down beside a woman perhaps fifteen years older, who greeted her with a quick, warm smile.

Runcorn noticed the movement of a man a couple of rows in front of him because he turned to stare at the girl with an intensity unsuitable in church. He was almost handsome, but for a tightness about his mouth. His features were regular and he had an excellent head of hair, thick with a slightly auburn tone to it. He was perhaps approaching forty.

If the girl were aware of his attention, she showed no sign of it at all; indeed, she seemed indifferent to any of the people around her except the vicar himself, who now appeared. He looked to be in his late forties, or perhaps a little more. He had a pale, ascetic face with a high brow and the same peat dark eyes as the girl in green. Almost immediately the

8

service commenced, with the usual soothing and familiar ritual. He conducted the proceedings sombrely and somewhat as if it were a habit he was so accustomed to that it required far less than his full attention. Runcorn began to wonder if there were any way in which he could escape the sermon without his boredom being rudely obvious, and concluded that there was not. Instead he would occupy his thoughts by looking at the people.

The man in front of Runcorn was looking at the girl again. There was too much emotion in his face to believe he was simply admiring her. He had to know her, and there had been conflict between them, at least on his part.

What of her? Runcorn could not see her now because she was facing forward, her attention on the vicar as he began his sermon. His subject was obedience, an easy matter for which to find plenty of reference, but not one so simple to give life or warmth to, or to make relevant to Christmas, now less than three weeks away. Runcorn wondered why on earth he had chosen it: it was singularly inappropriate. But then Runcorn did not know the congregation. There might be all kinds of passions running out of control that obedience could hold in check. The vicar might be the good shepherd trying all he knew to lead wayward sheep to safe pasture.

Barclay was also looking at the girl in green, and for a moment there was a hunger in his face that was quite unmistakable. Runcorn was almost embarrassed to have seen it.

Two men courting the same woman? Something that must happen in every village in England.

He had not been paying attention to the service. He had no idea what the curate had risen to do, only that his face was in every way different from that of the vicar. Where the older man was studious and disciplined, this man was mercurial and full of dreams. He seemed barely into his twenties, and yet there was a keen intelligence in him. He looked at the girl in green and smiled, then as if caught in a minor offence, quickly looked away. She turned a little, and Runcorn could see, even in the brief profile of her face, that she was smiling back, not wistfully as a lover, but with life and laughter, as a friend.

He would never know what tangle of emotions bound those people together. He had come because he thought Barclay would be here and, in spite of the absurdity of it, there was a chance he would see Melisande. He would like to think she was happy, whatever it was that had saddened her in London. The thought of her still facing some sort of darkness was so heavy inside him it was tight in his chest, like a physical band preventing him from taking a full breath. Where was she? He could not possibly ask Barclay if she was well. And any answer he gave would be no more than a formality. You did not discuss health or happiness with tradesmen, and he had made it abundantly clear that that was how he regarded Runcorn, and all police: the refuse collectors of society. He had said as much.

The congregation rose again to sing another hymn. The organist was good and the music pealed out with a powerful, joyous melody. Runcorn enjoyed singing. His voice was rich and he knew how to carry a tune.

It was as he sat down again, a moment or two after the people to the left of him, that he saw Melisande. She was nowhere near Barclay, but it was unmistakably her. He could never forget her face, the gentleness in it, the clear eyes, the laughter and the pain so near the surface.

She looked at him now with sudden, wide amazement. She smiled, and then self-consciously turned away.

Runcorn's heart lurched, the room swayed around him and he sat down in the pew so hard the woman in front turned to glare at him.

Melisande was here! And she remembered him! That smile was far more than just the acknowledgement of a stranger caught staring at her. It was more than civility; it had had warmth. He could feel it burn inside him.

The rest of the service passed by him in a blur of sound, beautiful and meaningless, like the splashes of colour the sunlight painted through the windows.

Afterwards he stood outside in the bright winter stillness as the congregation emerged, talking to each other, shaking the vicar by the hand, milling around exchanging gossip and good wishes.

Someone recognised him as a stranger and invited him to be introduced. He moved forward without thought as to what he was going to say, and found himself shaking the hand of the Reverend Arthur Costain, and offering his name without police rank.

'Welcome to Anglesey, Mr Runcorn,' Costain said with a smile. 'Are you staying with us over Christmas, or perhaps we may hope you will be with us longer?'

In that instant Runcorn made his decision. Melisande and Barclay already knew his profession, but he would tell no one else. He was not ashamed of it, but knowledge that he was a policeman made many people uncomfortable, and their defence was to avoid him.

'I will stay as long as I can,' he replied. 'Certainly until the New Year.'

Costain seemed pleased. 'Excellent. Perhaps you will call at the vicarage some time. My wife and I would be delighted to make your better acquaintance.' He indicated the woman beside him, and with whom the girl in green had sat during the service. Closer to, she was more interesting than his first glance had suggested. She was nothing like as beautiful as the younger woman, but there was a strength in her face that was unusual, full of both humour and sadness. Runcorn found it instantly pleasing, and accepted the invitation, only then realising that the vicar, at least, had said it as a matter of form. Runcorn blushed at his own foolishness.

It was Mrs Costain who rescued him. 'Forgive my husband, Mr Runcorn. He is always hoping for new parishioners. We shall not press you into staying beyond your pleasure, I assure you. Is this your first visit to the island?'

He recognised her kindness with surprise. He was not used to such acceptance from people of her social class. He had lost his sense of where Melisande was in the crowd, but he knew precisely where Barclay was standing, only yards away, looking at him with distaste. How long would it be before he told Mrs Costain that Runcorn was a policeman?

But Barclay was not looking at Runcorn. He was staring at the girl in green, his eyes intent on her face so Runcorn wondered how she was not aware of it, even uncomfortable. There was a brooding emotion in him that seemed both longing and anger, and when the man with auburn hair, who had also watched her, approached, his face tight and bitter, for an instant the tension between her and Barclay was so palpable that others were momentarily uncomfortable as well.

'Morning, Newbridge.' Barclay's voice was curt.

'Morning, Barclay,' the auburn-haired man replied. 'Pleasant weather.'

Everyone else was silent.

'I doubt it will last,' Barclay responded.

'Do you imagine we will have a white Christmas?' Costain put in quickly.

Barclay's eyebrows rose. 'White?' he said sarcastically, as if the word held a dozen other, more pungent meanings. 'Hardly.'

13

The girl in green swung round to look at him with amusement and then a sudden little shiver, hunching her shoulders as though she were cold, although she was well dressed and there was no wind.

'Olivia?' Costain said anxiously.

'Don't fuss,' his wife's voice was soft. Had Runcorn not been standing so close he would not have heard her.

Costain was disconcerted. He looked from one to the other of them and did not know how to address the deeper meaning that was understood between them.

Barclay nodded curtly and walked over towards Melisande, waiting for him on the path by the lich-gate. Runcorn watched him, and for a moment his eyes met Melisande's and he was unaware of anyone else. Newbridge brushed past him, said something to Olivia and she replied, her voice cool and light. Her words were courteous, her face almost empty of expression. She did not like him; Runcorn was certain of it in that instant.

He thanked Mrs Costain for her kindness, glanced briefly at the others in acknowledgement, then excused himself and went in the opposite direction. He made his way across the graveyard between the carved angels and the funeral urns and the headstones, and into the shadow of the yew trees beyond. He walked out of the further gate into the road, his mind still whirling.

It was his profession to watch people and read reactions. There was so much more to investigate than the words given in answer. It was as much the way they were said, the hesitations, the angle of the head, the movement and the stillness that told him of the passions beneath. That small group in the churchyard had been torn by emotions too powerful to control except with intense effort. The air was heavy, tingling on the skin like that before the breaking of a storm.

Did everybody else know it too, or was it just he? In spite of his separateness, his observation of the situation so intellectually cool, he was as much a victim as any of them. He was just as human, as vulnerable and every bit as absurd. What could be more ridiculous than the way he felt about Melisande, a woman to whom he could never be more than a public servant she had been able to assist, because it was the right thing and she had had the courage to do so, in spite of her brother's disapproval?

He went back to Mrs Owen's house because he knew she had cooked Sunday dinner for him and it would be a graceless thing not to return and eat it, in spite of the fact he felt already as if the comfortable walls of the house would close him in almost unbearably. And the last thing he wanted was trivial conversation, no matter how well meant. But he was a man of habit, and he had learned painfully the cost of bad manners.

He had an excuse to leave quickly: the weather was exceptionally pleasant for December, and he determined to walk as far as he could and still return by dusk. The wild, lonely paths along the shore, with the turbulent noise of breaking water and screaming gulls, fitted his mood perfectly. It was nature eternal and far beyond man's control. It was an escape to become part of it, simply by hearing the sounds, feeling the wind in his face and looking at the limitless horizon. It was big enough, and that comforted him. He saw in it a kind of truth.

The next day he walked the shore all the way from Beaumaris, north and east to Penmon Point. He stood and stared at the lighthouse and Puffin Island beyond. The day after he went all the way past the Menai Bridge until he could see the great towers of Caernarfon Castle on the opposite shore, and the vast, white-crowned peaks of Snowdonia. The following day he did the same, walking until he was exhausted.

Even so, he no longer slept well. The next morning he rose early, shaved and dressed, and went outside into the winter dawn. The air had a hard edge of ice on it, so sharp he gasped as he breathed it in. But he found a perverse pleasure in it also. It was clean and bitter, and he imagined he could see the distances it had blown across, the dark, glimmering water and the starlight.

Without realising it he had walked uphill towards the church again. Its tower loomed massive against the paling sky. He went in through the lich-gate and up the path, then round through the graveyard, picking his way across the grass crisp with frost. The dawn was sending up pale shafts of light in the east and throwing shadows from the gravestones and the occasional marble angel.

Perhaps that was why he was almost on the body before he realised what it was. She was lying at the base of a carved cross, her white gown crisp with hoarfrost, her face stiff, her black hair in a cloud around her like shadow. Only the blood drenching the lower half of her body was flooding scarlet with the strengthening daylight.

Runcorn was too horrified to move. He stood staring at her as if he had seen an apparition and if he waited his vision would clear and it would vanish. But the cold moved into his bones, the fingers of light crept around further, and she remained as terribly real. He knew who she was. Olivia Costain, the girl in green who had walked up the aisle of the church as if on a grassy lea.

Runcorn moved at last, going forward to bend on to one knee and touch her freezing hand. It was more than cold; the fingers were locked. Her eyes were wide open. Even here, like this, something of her beauty remained, a delicacy to the bones that wrenched inside him with pity for what she had been.

He looked down at the terrible wound in her stomach, clotted with thick blood, the flesh itself hidden. She must have been standing close to the grave, with her back to the cross, facing whoever it was that had done this to her. She had not been running away. He studied the ground and saw no damage to the grass except what he himself had done, bending over her. There was nothing to say she had fought, no marks on either of her hands, or on her arms or throat. Her killer could not have taken her by surprise from behind. They had stood face to face and the attack must have been sudden and terrible.

From such an injury she would have bled to death very quickly – in just moments, he hoped. It was bright arterial blood, the force of life. Surely it would not be possible to stand close enough to someone and inflict such a blow without being stained by blood oneself?

Runcorn stepped back and automatically cast his eyes about for the weapon. He did not expect to find it, but he must be certain. He could see nothing, no trace of red in the white daylight, no irregularity in the frost-pale grass, except the way he himself had come, as both she and her killer must have also, before the dew was iced hard.

This was close to the shortest day of the year and it was already late enough for people to be about. He must find someone to watch the body, keep anyone else from disturbing it. He must report it to the local police. At the very least he must prevent Costain from seeing her himself.

He found the sexton sombre and discreet, and asked him to stand guard, then followed his directions to the cottage of Police Sergeant Warner, who would still be at home at this hour.

Warner was just finishing his breakfast and his wife was

reluctant to disturb him until she saw Runcorn's face in the inside light, and the shock in his eyes. Then she made no demur. She passed him a cup of tea and insisted he drink it while he explained his errand to Warner himself, a large, soft-spoken man in his early forties.

'I suppose you'll be used to this, coming from London, an' all,' he said a little huskily, after Runcorn had described the scene to him, and the little he had deduced from it. 'I never dealt with murder before, 'cepting as you'd call a fight that ended badly murder.' He did not mean it insultingly. His face was filled not only with sorrow but with a kind of help-lessness as the enormity of his own task dawned on him. Runcorn could see his fear.

'If I can help,' he offered, and immediately wondered if he had trespassed already, implying, however obliquely, that the local force was inferior. He regretted it, but it was too late.

Warner swallowed. 'Well, we'll be getting someone from the mainland, no doubt,' he said quickly. 'Maybe the chief constable, or such. But I'd be mighty grateful if you'd lend a hand until then, seeing as you have the experience.'

'Of course,' Runcorn agreed. 'First thing, someone'll have to tell her family, and as soon as possible; get a doctor to look at her. Then we should have her put somewhere decent.'

'Yes.' Warner looked bewildered. 'Yes, I'll do that. Poor vicar.' He pushed his hand up over his brow, blinking rapidly. 'What a terrible thing to happen.' He glanced at Runcorn hopefully. 'I suppose it couldn't be an accident of some kind? Could she have . . . fell, somehow?

'No,' Runcorn said simply. He did not bother to go over the details again, or even mention the absurdity of Olivia Costain walking alone at night in the graveyard carrying a knife large enough to cause an injury like the one he had seen. She had not tripped, she had fallen backwards from the weight of the assault. The blade had not been found.

Warner sighed, his face pale but flushed unnaturally across the cheek, his eyes downcast. 'Sorry, I just . . .' He looked up again suddenly. 'We aren't used to this kind o' thing here. Known Miss Olivia since she were . . . little. Who'd do this to her?'

'We have to find that out,' Runcorn said simply. 'It's where our duty gets hard and ugly, and it matters we do it right.'

Warner rose to his feet, scraping the kitchen chair on the floor as he pushed it back. 'I'll go an' tell the vicar, an' Mrs Costain. She'll be torn to bits. They were very close, she an' Miss Olivia, more like real sisters they were, not just in-law, like. Will you . . . will you go and fetch Dr Trimby? His house is hard to find; my wife'll take you. Then I'd better get a message to the inspector in Bangor, and no doubt he'll be sending for Sir Alan Faraday from Caernarfon.'

Runcorn accepted without argument. A few moments later he was walking beside Mrs Warner as she led him through a hasty short cut across the road and through one backstreet after another until they arrived at the door of Dr Trimby's house. It was now nearly nine o'clock on a gusty morning, the streets were busy, and there were three or four people already waiting in his surgery.

Trimby's name did not suit him. He was short and stocky, with flyaway hair, a shirt that defied the iron and a cravat as unfashionable as it was possible to be. Nothing of his apparel matched anything else. However, his attention was instant and complete. Once Mrs Warner had told him who Runcorn was, he listened with grief and total concentration. He made no notes at all, but Runcorn had no doubt that he remembered every detail. His blunt, asymmetric face was heavy with sadness.

'I suppose you'd better take me to her,' he said, hauling himself to his feet. On the way out he picked up his bag, good leather once, but now bearing the scars of twenty years of service in all weathers.

They walked back up to the graveyard roughly the way Runcorn had come with Mrs Warner, and found the sexton still standing guard alone and shivering with cold.

Trimby looked past him at the body and his face bleached so pale Runcorn was afraid for a moment that he was going to collapse. But he made a painfully intense effort, and regained his composure. He bent and began to make his professional examination.

Runcorn excused the sexton and waited quietly in the rising wind, growing colder and colder as the minutes passed.

Finally Trimby stood up awkwardly, his legs stiff from kneeling, his balance a little uncertain.

'No later than midnight,' his voice was hoarse. He coughed and began again. 'Far as I can tell from the rigor mortis. But you can see that yourself with the frost, I expect. Cold, exposure makes a difference. Look for whoever saw her last, if you can trust them. Can't . . . can't make a wound like that without getting blood on yourself. She didn't fight.' His voice broke and he took a long, difficult moment to regain his self-control. 'Nothing much else I can tell you. Can't learn anything more from this. I'll get her out of here, get her . . . decent.' He turned to go.

'Doctor . . .' Runcorn called out.

Trimby waved a hand at him impatiently. 'You can see as much as I can. This is your business, not mine.' He continued to walk rapidly between the gravestones.

Runcorn's legs were longer and he caught up with him. 'It's not all you can tell me,' he said, matching his step to Trimby's. 'You know her – tell me something about her. Who would have done this?'

'A raving madman!' Trimby snapped back without turning to look at him or slacken his pace.

Runcorn snatched his arm and pulled him up short, swinging him round a little. It was a thing he had never done before in all the violent and tragic cases he had ever dealt with. His own emotions were more deeply wrenched than he had imagined. 'No, it was not a madman,' he said savagely.

'It was someone she knew and was not afraid of. You know that as well as I do. She was facing him, she wasn't running away, and she didn't fight back because she wasn't expecting him to strike her. Why was she here anyway? Who would she meet in a graveyard alone, late at night?'

Trimby stared at him, angry and defensive. 'What kind of world do you live in where a man who would do that to a woman is considered sane?' he asked, his voice trembling.

Runcorn saw the profound emotion in him, the bewilderment and the sense of loss far deeper than he felt from the expected deaths he must encounter in his practice from time to time. Olivia had presumably been his patient and he might have known her all her life. He answered honestly. 'When we say "madman", we mean someone unknown to us, who acts without reason, attacking at random, someone outside the world we understand. This wasn't someone like that, and I think you know it.'

Trimby lowered his gaze. 'If there were anything I could tell you, I would,' he replied. 'I have no idea who it was, or why. That is your job to find out, God help you.' And he turned and strode away through the last of the gravestones, leaving Runcorn alone, cold, and spattered by the first heavy drops of rain.

It was a long and miserable day of small duties before Runcorn finally met again with Warner and told him what Trimby had said, confirming his own deduction. The medical evidence, such as it was, added nothing that was of help. Olivia Costain had been stabbed in the stomach with a broad blade. The single thrust had severed the artery and she had bled to death within moments, falling backwards from where she had been standing. As Runcorn had supposed, there were no defensive wounds on her hands or arms, or anywhere else on her body.

'She probably died before midnight,' he finished.

Warner looked tired, his eyes red-rimmed as if he had been sleepless far longer than one interminable day. They sat at the same kitchen table as this morning, again with a pot of tea between them.

'I told the vicar,' Warner said miserably. 'Poor man was shattered. I think Mrs Costain took it even harder. Very close, they were.'

'Did you find out who was the last to see Miss Costain alone?' Runcorn asked, bringing him back to the facts. He had seen young constables profoundly shaken by death. The first few times were the hardest, especially when the victim was peculiarly vulnerable, young or old, or in some other way helpless. It helped to concentrate on the little they could do now that was of use.

Warner looked up. 'Oh. Yes. Housekeeper saw her leave at about ten, or a few minutes after. Said she was just going for a walk. Seems she did that quite often, walked alone, even after dark. Didn't go far.'

'So there are two hours during which she could have been killed?'

'Yes, seems like it,' Warner agreed. 'I asked everyone where they were. Not a lot of help. The vicar was in his study, Mrs Costain was in the library reading until she went to bed at about eleven. Their neighbours in the big house up the road – which would be Mr John Barclay and his sister, Mrs Ewart, widow so they say – he went out to visit a friend, but he walked home alone and didn't disturb the servants when he got in. So there's no proof where he was after about half-past ten. She was in bed, but she dismissed her maid, so we've only her word.' Warner looked more and more unhappy. 'And the curate, Kelsall, lives alone in a little cottage half a mile away. Mr Newbridge, who had been courting Miss Costain until recently, lives about two miles away, and he was working in his study until eleven. But he dismissed his manservant after dinner, so we have only his word also.'

'Reasonable,' Runcorn admitted reluctantly. 'I couldn't account for myself either. A late walk on a clear winter evening is a natural thing to do. Have a look at the stars. You can really see them here. And most people let their servants go if there's no need to keep them up. Anybody see her after that? See anybody about, or hear anything? What about servants, courting maybe? Any neighbours up?'

Warner shook his head. 'Asked anywhere I knew of, Mr Runcorn, and not a thing I can see as helps us at all. All the other neighbours so far can say where they were, 'cos they all have families, or servants as saw them. Not that they all knew Miss Costain that well, except in passing, as it were. Terribly shaken up, they were. We've never had anything like that here. It's . . .' he stopped, lost for words.

He shook his head slowly, avoiding Runcorn's eyes. 'Got a message, chief constable's going to be here some time late tomorrow. He'll take over then. Can't say as I'm sorry. This is not the kind of thing I know how to handle, Mr Runcorn. The odd robbery now and then, even a barn burning or a real bad fight I can deal with, but this is different. Got everybody frightened, and sick with grief, it has. Glad enough to have Sir Alan take charge of it. But then I'm obliged to you for your help. We'll hand over a tidy investigation, evidence all straight and done right, thanks to you.' He smiled very slightly, his shoulders easing a little, his colour ashen as if at last he could let go of some of the burden that he had carried today. 'I'm sure Sir Alan would want to thank you himself, but for us here, I'm grateful, Mr Runcorn.'

Runcorn knew it would be this way. He had no jurisdiction in Anglesey, no standing beyond that of any other responsible citizen. And yet he felt absurdly disappointed. It was not that he wanted work. The case was tragic, nothing about it was obvious, and he certainly had no idea who could have murdered Olivia Costain, or why. But he wanted to see it to the end, he wanted to find out who had destroyed a young woman who had been uniquely alive and full of grace. And perhaps also he had wanted to be of value, here so very close to Melisande, not merely another onlooker. Dealing with violence and fear was the one thing he was good at. It was where his skills were treasured.

But of course the chief constable was coming. It was too grave a case for him not to. It was not even twenty-four hours since the murder, and panic was rising, fear, cold and dark, wakening like the wind rattling at the windows. Except that the wind could be shut out, and fear entered in spite of all the locks and bars in the world.

'Glad to help,' Runcorn said quietly. 'Sorry it wasn't more.'

Warner held out his hand suddenly. 'Very glad you were here, Mr Runcorn. Very glad.'

Runcorn took it. There did not seem any more to add, and now he would leave to be alone, face the fact that he did not belong here as he walked down the incline towards Mrs Owen's house, and another night before an empty day.

But in spite of his resolution, by mid-afternoon Runcorn walked back towards Warner's house, past the field where the redwings were still busy. It was a brisk afternoon with high-scudding clouds and occasional, freezing showers, the light glittering bright. Runcorn was hungry for information. He knew it was foolish because the sergeant could not tell him anything. It was no longer Runcorn's concern; he was not one of them. The reminder was painful. It forced him to realise more vividly an emptiness inside himself, a growing need for something more than he had.

As he passed the entrance to the churchyard, memory and grief clenched inside him again, making him even colder. He was surprised to see John Barclay ahead of him walking beside a man almost his own height. He was bareheaded even in this wind, and his hair was thick and fair. He had an almost military precision to his step, and even at a distance Runcorn could see the elegance in the cut of his clothes. It had to be Sir Alan Faraday, the chief constable. But why was he talking so closely to Barclay, as if they were friends?

Runcorn stopped, and perhaps the unexpected action caught Barclay's eye, because he put his arm on Faraday and said something, and both of them turned towards Runcorn. Barclay took the first step forward, and there was something obscurely threatening in his action.

Runcorn stood his ground.

'Good afternoon,' Barclay said quite loudly, speaking when they were still several yards distant. 'Runcorn, isn't it?'

'Good afternoon, Mr Barclay,' Runcorn replied, still not moving.

Closer to, the other man was good-looking, his eyes were steady and a remarkable blue.

'This is the London fellow I was mentioning,' Barclay told him. 'Runcorn gave us a hand before you could get here.' He looked at Runcorn. 'Sir Alan Faraday, Chief Constable of the County. Obviously this is in his hands now. Very serious case indeed. Warrants the highest attention, I think, before the horror of it can cause public fear and unrest. But we're obliged to you for your help in the beginning.'

'Indeed,' Faraday affirmed, watching cautiously. 'Very good of you to step in so professionally. It seems you've left all the evidence well ordered for us. Very nasty case, and of course people are terrified. It looks as if we have a lunatic on the island. We must do all we can to reassure them, and see that panic does not take hold.'

Runcorn was at a loss to know how to respond graciously, and without allowing his emotions to betray him. It was at times like this he wished desperately that he had more polish, more of the assurance of a gentleman that would have him assume he was in the right, regardless, and then others would assume it also. Instead he felt like a good servant being dismissed for the night. And yet to resent it would make him absurd.

But he was absurd. It stung, it was humiliating. Monk would have known how to carry it off with such flair that they would have been the ones to feel foolish. But he was not Monk, he was not clever with words, above all he had no grace, no elegance.

'You are welcome to such help as I can give, Sir Alan,' he replied instead, and heard himself sound as if he were indeed a servant asking for approval.

Faraday nodded. 'Good of you,' he said briefly. 'We should be able to find the fellow soon enough. Small place, and all that. Decent people. Terrible tragedy, just before Christmas.'

Barclay looked at Faraday. 'I'd like a word with Runcorn, if you don't mind. I'll meet you up at the vicarage in a moment or two.'

Faraday acknowledged with a brief nod towards Runcorn, and within moments he was fifty yards away, walking easily as if miles would have meant little to him.

'Good man,' Barclay observed with satisfaction. 'Ex-army, of course. He'll sort this out, calm people's fears and get us back to something like normal. Can't undo the memory or the loss, but no one could do that. You can't help any more, Runcorn. These are not your people, not the class you are used to dealing with. I'm sure you mean well, but you won't understand them, or their ways.'

Runcorn wished to say something, but everything that came to his mind sounded to him as if he were trying to defend himself. He remained standing silently in the wind, the grief of the churchyard, the reality of death and loss overwhelming. He should not give even a passing thought to his own feelings.

'As long as you find who killed Miss Costain, it hardly matters who does it,' he retaliated.

'My dear fellow, of course it matters!' Barclay said hotly, but with a continued smile on his face, more of a pulling back of the lips to show perfect teeth. 'We cannot help the dead, but the feelings of the living matter very much. Our conduct can make an enormous difference to their fear, their sense of danger and disorder. But what I really wanted to say to you, privately from Faraday, is that he is an excellent man, and very soon to become engaged to marry my sister, Mrs Ewart, who as you may recall is widowed.' His eyes did not waver from Runcorn's face. 'It is a most fortunate match and will offer her everything she wishes. I hope I do not have to spell out in detail how unfortunate it would be if you were to mention your past professional involvement in London, however innocently intended. It can only raise questions and require explanations it would be wiser to leave unsaid. So please do not force yourself to her attention by making apparent that you have a past acquaintance, however superficial.'

Runcorn felt as if he had been slapped so hard the breath was momentarily knocked out of him. He drew in some air, and found nothing to say in return, not a word that touched the wound in him.

'I knew you'd understand,' Barclay said blithely. 'Hope this wretched matter is all ended rather faster than you dealt with the other business. What a mess! Still, this seems clearer. I'm obliged to you. Good day.' And without waiting for Runcorn to think of a reply, he turned and followed after the way Faraday had gone.

The next two days passed in a chaotic unhappiness as Faraday took over all that Runcorn had left, of course with the help of Warner, who had no choice in such matters. He reminded Runcorn of the past when Monk had been in the Metropolitan

Police with him, years ago. Monk was always cleverer, always so sure of himself, at least on the surface. Of course Runcorn had not known then of the private ghosts and demons that haunted him. His own blindness had seen nothing but the iron-hard grace of the mask with which Monk protected himself. But if Faraday had anything of Monk's complexity, Runcorn found no trace of it in his smooth face, no wound in the eyes, no leap of the mind to understand more passionately than others.

Runcorn would have been glad if Faraday had had Monk's skill. More than any rivalry, any personal importance at all, it mattered that they find who had killed Olivia Costain. And he realised with a rising sickness in his stomach that they must also prevent him from killing anyone else, any other unique and lovely woman who was vulnerable, challenging, and at heart alone – such as Melisande. That was the core of his fear, and for that he would sacrifice any dignity or personal pride, any ambition whatever.

But two days went by and, as far as he could tell, or hear from a fearful Mrs Owen, no progress at all was made. Whenever they could, people remained in their homes. After dark the streets were deserted, even though there was no snow yet, and the wind no fiercer or colder than before. There were whispers of madness, even of something loose that was less than human, some creature of the dark to harrow and destroy before the light of Christmas when hope returned to the world.

Runcorn passed Trimby in the street, still looking as untidy as before. He was striding out, his coat-tails flying, his hat abandoned and his hair streaming out like a wind-blown banner, and he went by without speaking, consumed in his own thoughts.

Runcorn could bear it no longer. He went to the vicarage where he knew Faraday would be, and found him speaking to writers and journalists from the island, and from mainland Wales as far away as Denbigh and Harlech.

No one took any notice as one more man pushed his way into the crowded withdrawing room, and he was asked to stand at the back and listen while Faraday did his best to dispel the fear rising with every new question. What kind of a lunatic was loose among them? Had there been sightings? When? Where? By whom? Could somebody be sheltering this creature? Did the vicar have any opinions? Why had Olivia Costain been the victim?

Faraday kept on trying to soothe the fear, and to the last question he answered so decisively that Olivia was an exemplary young woman, known and loved in the community, and of an unblemished reputation, that his very vehemence suggested doubt.

When Runcorn spoke to him later, alone, his words conformed to that opinion. They were in the room Costain had set apart for Faraday's use, a quiet morning room with a good fire burning, and walls either crowded with books, or hung with an odd jumble of paintings, cartoons and drawings. There were papers spread over the table and a pen and ink well beside them.

'It wasn't a madman,' Runcorn said grimly. 'You know that, sir. The evidence says it was someone she knew.' He remained standing, too angry to sit, although in truth he had not been invited to do so.

'No,' Faraday agreed unhappily. 'At least, I appreciate that she knew him, but I think it's not wise to say so.' He looked up at Runcorn intently. 'I hope you will have the decency not to speak irresponsibly? It will only increase the fear there is already. As long as people think it is someone they don't know, at least they are not turning upon each other.' He seemed to be concerned that Runcorn understood. 'There is a sense of unity, a willingness to help. That is why I am not saying that she was a difficult young woman with some very unsatisfactory ideas, even dangerous in a way. Poor Costain had his troubles with her. She appeared to be unwilling to settle down. She refused several very good offers of marriage, and it looked as if she were not prepared to become adult and accept her role in society. She expected her brother to keep her indefinitely, while she drifted from one rather foolish dream to another. Her virtue had not yet been questioned openly, but it was only a matter of time before that happened, which is hard for any man, but especially so for one in his position.'

Thoughts raged through Runcorn's mind, memories of Olivia walking up the aisle of the church with the same careless grace she might have trodden the beach, the foam breaking around her, the wind off the sea in her face. Why should she marry to suit her brother's social or religious life? Then he realised he was thinking in his mind of Melisande marrying Faraday to suit Barclay's ambition, and to free him from responsibility for her.

He looked at Faraday, straight-backed, good-looking, unimaginative, comfortable. Did he love Melisande? Did he adore her, see in her the unique courage and grace, the kindness strong enough to defy convention and risk her own safety to give witness to a crime, as she had done for Monk and Runcorn when they had been pursuing the assassin of the sewers in London? Did he care desperately that she was happy, that nothing in her was forced, crushed, distorted into duty rather than belief? Or was she just a lovely and very suitable wife, one of whom he need never be anxious or ashamed, one who would fit all his social and political ambitions?

That was what Barclay wanted for her: never to be in want or need in the conventional sense, to be respected, even envied, to be secure for the rest of her life. In many ways perhaps that was more than most women could expect. And yet Runcorn, who could offer her nothing but admiration, was incensed for her. He wanted her to have so much more than that.

It was impertinent of him, and arrogant. Perhaps she was realistic, and for her it would be sufficient.

He finished the rest of his conversation with Faraday hardly knowing what he was saying, except that at the end he was dismissed knowing little more than he had when he came in. There was fear and confusion everywhere, and Faraday was, so far, at a loss to know where to proceed next. His knowledge of men and events, his ability to command, did not extend to anything like this.

Runcorn walked alone, right along the south shore of the island, over rocks and sand, always watching the tide, aware of its danger. The sea was both provider and destroyer; it granted no mercy to anyone. He had read that somewhere. Looking at its constantly shifting surface, its power, its beauty and deceit, he believed it absolutely.

He walked until he could see the towers of Caernarfon across the Strait. Then he rested a short while and walked back again through occasional rain. The wind was behind him, but even so, he was exhausted and it was close to dark when, without thought, his feet took him back to walk up towards the churchyard. He knew why. Barclay and Melisande were staying in the big house beyond the green, with Sir Alan Faraday as their guest. If there was anywhere he might catch a glimpse of her, it was here.

It was a quarter of an hour later when he was watching the light fade across the water that he heard her voice behind him. Her footsteps had been soundless on the grass.

'Mr Runcorn?'

He swung round, his breath catching in his throat. He had

difficulty answering her. She was wearing a dark gown and a cloak over it with a hood against the wind. The amber light from the last of the sun was soft on her face, accentuating the bones of her cheeks and the line of her chin. He had never seen anyone so beautiful, or so able to hope, to care, and to be hurt.

'Good evening, Mrs Ewart,' he said hoarsely.

'I am glad you are here,' she answered. 'Sir Alan is a good man, and I suppose John was right to send for him . . .' She hesitated. 'But I don't believe he has the experience of . . . of a terrible crime like this to be able to learn quickly enough what happened, and who is responsible.'

Should he try to comfort her? He could see the fear in her eyes. She was right, Faraday had no idea how to investigate a murder. It was not really what chief constables were for. He was doing it because Melisande was here, and perhaps because the crime had raised such terror on the island people were close to panic. The brutality of it was something they had never experienced before.

Should he lie to her?

'Quickly enough?' he questioned. 'Do you fear it will happen again?' Why had he asked her that? It was no comfort at all.

'Won't it?' she said softly. 'You know about these things. Does somebody do this once and then stop? Won't they defend themselves, if we get close to them, if we seem to be about to tear the mask off and show who they really are?'

He shivered in spite of himself. Her fear touched him more cruelly than the dusk wind. She was right, the only safety lay in swiftness. Strike before the victim knew the direction of the blow, and strike fatally. He longed to be able to protect her, but he had no duty, no place here at all.

'Won't they?' she repeated. 'Have I placed you in an impossible position?' She looked away from him. 'I am very afraid that we are out of our depth. Sir Alan is speaking as if the killer is some random beast come out of the wild places in the centre of the island, the hills beyond our climbing.' She stopped abruptly, biting her lower lip, afraid to say the rest of what was crowding her mind.

Runcorn said it for her. 'But you think the beast comes from within one of us here in the houses and streets we think we know?'

Her eyes opened wide and there was a warmth in them, even a kind of relief. 'Don't you? Please be honest with me, Mr Runcorn. This is too terrible for us to be exchanging lies because we think they are easier. Olivia deserves better than that, and for our own sakes we can't afford to keep looking the other way.'

Why did she think so? She had not seen the body as he had. What had she heard or felt, that she understood this? Who was she afraid for? Did she know who it was, or perhaps suspect? She knew Costain and his wife, and of course she knew her brother. She had been fond of Olivia, so it was possible she had learned from her something of Newbridge,

38

or even of the curate Kelsall. Was she afraid the investigation would expose things that were ugly in any of them, or all?

Everyone had actions, wounds they were ashamed of, secrets they would fight to protect. Someone might even have lashed out to protect the memory of Olivia herself. Grief could do many violent things no one could foresee, even in those most affected. Sometimes it deepened love, other times it broke it.

'Have you told Sir Alan your fears?' Runcorn hated even mentioning the man's name.

Melisande shook her head fractionally. 'No. I think he has enough to worry about, with the feeling that's growing among people, and their demands for help, and for a solution. Nobody can just . . . produce it, because it's needed. We are not children to have all our fears soothed away. Something terrible has happened, and Alan cannot undo it for us, or provide the answers we want.' Distress, and something like pity touched her face. 'I don't suppose anyone can.'

Was she meaning only what she said – that they must all endure it because there was no other way, and it was unfair to expect it? Was she defending Faraday? Or saying he could not handle the task? Or both? Runcorn struggled to read her eyes, the line of her lips, but it was too dark to see clearly any more, and he did not understand anyway.

He knew she was afraid, but then only a fool would not be. Whatever the truth was, it would bring pain. Their lives would never heal over the things they would hear of each other, the shortcomings, the secrets ordinary life could have left decently covered. Murder swept all that away.

Did she love Faraday? The helplessness and the mercy of it was that one did not have to be perfect to be loved, one did not even have to be especially good. It was a gift, a grace. He had never tested it himself. He was clumsy, ungenerous, not knowing how to respond.

He longed now to say something that would comfort her, be of more help in the days ahead, which would hold pain for her, but all he could do was tell her the truth. He wanted to protect her from it, most of all from the actual danger. It was the one skill he had, and he was unable to use it because this was not his jurisdiction. He had no more authority here than the postman or the fishmonger – less, because he did not belong.

'Mr Runcorn . . .' she said tentatively.

'Yes?'

'You found Olivia's body, didn't you?' It was not really a question. She was leading to something further.

'Yes.' The misery of it was in his voice.

'Do you think she was killed by a madman, someone none of us know?'

He hesitated.

'Please?' she said urgently. 'This is no time for comfortable lies. Do not treat me as if I were foolish. Olivia was my friend. I really cared for her very much, even though I knew her well only a short time. We . . . we had much in common. I would like to know the truth, and Alan will not tell me.'

'Then . . .' he started, and stopped. She was inviting him to tell her something that the man she was going to marry had refused to.

'Your silence is answer.' She turned away from him, her voice tight with disappointment.

He could not bear it. 'No, it was someone she knew,' he admitted. 'She was facing him, not running away.'

She looked at him again, her eyes filled with grief. 'Poor Olivia. Can you think of anything more terrible? I want to ask you if she felt much pain, but I am not sure if I can endure the answer.'

'No,' he said quickly. 'It can only have been a few moments at most.'

'Thank you.' Her voice was soft. 'I'm sorry to have . . . Mr Runcorn, will you please help us? I don't think we know how to deal with this. We are not used to such . . . discomfort of the mind, such feelings of pain and fear when we don't know what to do.'

He was stunned, and yet this was exactly what he had wanted, to help! Had she any idea what she asked of him? He had no authority, no rights here at all. Faraday would resent it. Barclay would be furious. He should tell her that, explain all the reasons why he could not do it. Instead, he simply said, 'Yes, of course I will.'

'Thank you.' The faintest smile softened her mouth for a

moment. 'I am very grateful. I should not have kept you standing here in the cold so long. Good night, Mr Runcorn.' And slowly, with intense grace, she turned and walked away.

He was too overwhelmed to reply. He remained where he was, shivering in the wind until he could no longer see her figure in the shadows. Then at last he turned to go back to Mrs Owen's house.

There was only one obvious place to begin, and that was with Sergeant Warner. Runcorn was already sitting at Warner's kitchen table at eight o'clock, having risen when it was still dark and walked up the incline so that as soon as he could see the lamps lit, he could go in.

'Doing everything we can think of,' Warner said, offering Runcorn fresh, hot tea, which he accepted gratefully. The day was bitter, a raw wind edged with sleet blowing in from the east. 'Hard to know what to do next,' he went on, bending to open up the stove so the heat spread out into the room. He did not look at Runcorn. 'Porridge?' he asked.

'Thank you.' It had been too early to expect breakfast from Mrs Owen, and actually he had barely thought of it.

'I feel helpless,' Warner added, his voice full of misery.

Runcorn recognised it as an oblique way of telling him that Faraday was making no progress, and possibly had little idea what to do next. He had painted himself into something of a corner with his insistence that it was a madman. It was easy enough to understand why he had done so, faced with the brutality of the crime and the horror it had awoken in everyone, family and stranger alike. The whole town suffered under a weight of shock as if life had been darkened for all of them. Something irreparable had been destroyed.

Warner was too loyal to say outright that Faraday was floundering, in fact he would not even look Runcorn in the eye as he tried to find his way around it, but that was what he meant.

'He's going to have to acknowledge that it was someone she knew,' he conceded over the porridge making. 'Nobody'll want to think so, but you can't get away from it.' He stirred the pan a final time. 'Then you can start asking the questions that'll lead us to the truth.' His voice undoubtedly carried more confidence than he felt.

Warner ladled the porridge into two bowls and brought it to the table, along with milk and spoons, and both salt and sugar to add, as Runcorn wished. 'But what kind of questions?' He faced Runcorn fully now that the awkwardness of pretending he was not really looking for help had been negotiated.

They both started to eat while Runcorn thought carefully of how to reply. The porridge was thick and smooth and the more he ate, the more he liked it.

What should he say that was honest and still kept a remnant of tact? Did tact even matter any more at this point? Surely now the situation was harsh and dangerous enough that only the truth would serve? If he were taking over this case from someone else, what would he do, were he able to have complete control of it?

Warner was waiting for him to speak, his face pale with the deep exhaustion of fear.

'I'd be plain,' Runcorn told him quietly. 'There's not a lot of use going back over where everyone was because they've already said, and no one's going to admit to a lie. I suppose you haven't found the blade?'

Warner shook his head.

'It would have come from someone's kitchen,' Runcorn observed.

'We could see who's missing one?' Warner suggested doubtfully. 'But that'd mean pretty well saying as we thought it was one of them, or we couldn't even look.'

'And for all we know, it could've been washed and put back,' Runcorn added.

Warner winced, his face clearly mirroring his racing imagination: the Sunday joint carved with the weapon of murder.

Runcorn clenched his teeth. This was difficult, but he had promised Melisande that he would help, which meant that he must do so, wherever the truth led him, even to angering Faraday and possibly making an enemy of him. Neither would anyone else welcome the sort of questions that must be asked, but to investigate other than honestly would serve no purpose. However painful the truth of why Olivia had been killed, and by whom, it must be found. Along with that, inevitably, many other secrets, follies and shames would also be uncovered.

Perhaps even Melisande would be forced to see things it had been so much better to overlook. Very little would be the same afterwards.

Should he have warned her of that? Should he do so now? He knew the answer within himself. In the past he had some-times done what was expedient, said the right things, turned the occasional blind eye. It had won him the promotion Monk had never received. It had also earned him Monk's contempt and, if he were honest, his own as well. He could never have Melisande's love – it hurt to say so, a long, aching wound that would trouble him the rest of his life – but he would keep the integrity that made him able to look at her without shame.

'I don't know whether Sir Alan will look into the weapon more closely or not,' he said aloud to Warner. 'But what I would do, were it with me, is to learn more about Miss Costain herself, until I knew everything I could do about who really loved her, hated her. Who might have seen her as a threat, or a rival? And to do that I would also have to learn a lot more about her family and all those others who were part of her life.'

'I see,' Warner said slowly, thinking about what that could mean. He searched Runcorn's face, and saw there was no pretence in it, and no way of evading the truth. 'Then that's what we'll have to do, isn't it.' It was a statement. 'I've only dealt with fights and robberies before, and a little bit of embezzlement, a fire once. It was ugly. I expect this is going to be far worse. We'll need your help, Mr Runcorn.' This time there was a lift of doubt in his voice. He was asking as openly as he dared to.

For Runcorn the die was already cast: he had promised Melisande. Warner could add nothing to that. But he realised now that to investigate with any honesty he would have to go to Faraday and ask for his permission, which he had every right to refuse. Even the thought of facing him, pleading to be allowed to have a part in the case, clenched his stomach like a cramp. But he would be useless without approval. Of course, it would be simple enough to ask and be refused. Melisande would have to accept that. She would see Faraday's inadequacy and recognise it for the pride it was, and excuse Runcorn.

But would he excuse himself? Not even for an instant. Part of honesty would be using his skill to ask Faraday in such a way that he could not refuse. He had made enough mistakes in the past with clumsiness of words, lack of judgement, self-ishness, that he ought to have learned all the lessons by now. If he wanted to badly enough, he could place Faraday in a position where it would be impossible for him to refuse help. This was his one chance to be the man he had always failed to be in the past. He had let pride, anger and ambition stop him.

'I'll have to have Sir Alan's permission,' he said aloud to Warner, and saw his face cloud over instantly. 'I couldn't do it behind his back, even if I would like to.'

Warner shook his head. 'He'll likely not give it.'

'He might if I ask him the right way,' Runcorn explained. 'It'd be hard for him to say no in front of you, and whatever other men he has on the case, and perhaps the vicar as well? Even Mrs Costain. She was very close to Olivia. It would be hard to explain to her why he refused help.'

Warner's eyes widened with sudden understanding, and a new respect. 'Well, I'd never have thought of that,' he said slowly. 'Maybe I'll just have a word with Mrs Costain, and see as how that can be done. You're a clever man, Mr Runcorn, and I'm much obliged to have you on our side.'

So it was that evening that Runcorn walked up the incline through heavy rain beside Warner and they knocked at the vicarage door a few moments after Sir Alan Faraday had gone inside to inform Mr and Mrs Costain of his progress on the case. Warner was due to report also, so the housemaid did not hesitate to take their wet coats and show them both into the parlour where the others were gathered close to the fire.

Naomi Costain looked years older than she had a week ago. Her strong features were deeply marked by grief, her skin so pale she seemed pinched with cold, although the room was warm. She wore black, without ornament of any kind. It did not seem an ostentatious sign of mourning but simply as if she had not thought of it. Her hair was pinned up and kept out of her way, but it did not flatter her.

Costain himself sat on one of the other chairs, his clerical collar askew, his shoulders hunched. Faraday stood with military stiffness in front of the fire, successfully blocking it from anyone else, but apparently unaware of it. He, like Runcorn and Warner, must be feeling cold and wet. He stared at Warner with a lift of hope. Then, seeing Runcorn behind him, his expression closed over.

'Good evening,' he said tersely. 'Is there something we can do for you, Mr Runcorn?' He did not use his police rank, although he knew it.

There was no room for prevarication, Runcorn must either explain himself, or retreat. He felt foolish for having asked Warner to do this in front of Costain and his wife. Now his humiliation would be that much more public. Faraday could not afford to lose face in front of others. This had been a technical error, but it was too late to mend now. He chose his words as carefully as he could, something he was not used to doing.

'It appears to be a far more difficult case than it looked to begin with,' he said. 'I imagine that this close to Christmas, like everyone else, you are short-handed, especially of men used to dealing with crime.'

The silence was deafening. They were all staring at him, Costain with bewilderment, Naomi with hope, Faraday suspiciously.

'This is an island where there is very little crime,' Faraday replied. 'And even that is mostly the odd theft, or a fight that's more hot temper than cold violence.'

'Yes,' Costain agreed quickly. 'We . . . we've never had

anyone killed . . . so long as I've been here. We've never dealt with anything like this before. What . . . what do you advise?'

Faraday glared at him. It had been peculiarly tactless.

Runcorn knew to retreat. A word of pride or the slightest suggestion of professional superiority, and he would be excluded in such a way that there would be no room for Faraday to change his mind and ask him back.

'I don't know enough to advise,' he said hastily. 'All I meant to do was offer whatever help I can, as an extra pair of legs, so to speak.'

Faraday moved his weight from one foot to the other, still directly in front of the fire.

'Thank you,' Naomi said sincerely.

'To do what?' Faraday asked with an edge to his voice.

Runcorn hesitated. Was that a demand that he explain himself, or an oblique and defensive way of asking him for advice? He looked at Faraday. He was immaculately dressed, his thick hair neat. But there were hollow shadows smudged around his eyes and a tension in the way he stood that had little to do with the cold. He was in an unenviable position, and with a sudden surge of pity that startled and disconcerted him, Runcorn realised just how out of his depth Faraday was. He had never faced murder before, and people who were frightened and bewildered were looking to him for help he had no idea how to give.

'Ask some of the questions that may lead us towards whoever attacked Miss Costain,' he answered. He chose the

word 'attacked' as less brutal than 'murder', but no one in
the room was unaware of the reality.

Outside thunder rolled and the rain beat against the
windows.

'Of whom?' Faraday raised his eyebrows. 'We have already
spoken to all those who live anywhere near the graveyard.
Everyone in Beaumaris is appalled by what has happened.
They would all help, if they could.'

'No, sir.' Runcorn spoke before he had thought about it.
'At least one would not, and maybe many others.' He ignored
Faraday's scowl, and Costain's wave of denial. 'Not because
they know who is guilty,' he explained. 'For other reasons.
Everyone has things in their lives they would not share with
others: mistakes, embarrassments, events that are private, or
which might compromise someone they care for, or to whom
they owe a loyalty. It's natural to defend what privacy you
have. Everyone does.'

Costain sank back in his chair. Perhaps as a minister he
was beginning to understand.

Faraday stared. 'What are you suggesting, Runcorn? That
we dig into everyone's private lives?' He said it with immeas-
urable distaste.

Again Runcorn hesitated. How on earth could he answer
this without either offending Costain and his wife, or else
retreating until he lost whatever chance he had of investigating to any purpose at all? He knew the answer was to be
brutal, but he loathed doing it. Only the thought of Olivia

lying in the churchyard, soaked in her own blood, and his promise to Melisande, steeled him.

'Until you find the cause of this crime, yes I am,' he answered, meeting Faraday's blue eyes steadily. 'Murder is violent, ugly and tragic. There is no point investigating it as if it were the theft of a pair of fire dogs, or a set of silver spoons. It's the result of hatred or terror, not a moment of misplaced greed.'

Costain jerked back as if he had been hit.

'Really!' Faraday protested.

'Mr Runcorn is quite right,' Naomi said softly, but her voice was very clear in the quiet room. 'We must all put up with a little inconvenience or embarrassment if it is necessary to learn the truth. To do less would be despicably selfish. It is very good of you, Alan, to wish to protect us, and I appreciate your thoughtfulness, but we must face the truth.'

Faraday waited only a moment, then he turned again to Runcorn. He had no choice but to concede. He got it over with quickly. 'Yes. Yes, I regret it, but that does seem to be the situation. Perhaps it would be helpful if you were to give us some of your time, and most honourable of you, when I assume you are on holiday. Naturally I shall require you to report to me regularly, not only anything that you may feel you have learned, but also, of course, your intentions for the next step. I had better advise you what we have done so far, and where you should proceed.'

'Yes, sir,' Runcorn said quietly. He had no intention whatsoever of taking instructions from Faraday, who was obviously as concerned with appearances and order as with the darker sides of truth.

Faraday turned to Costain. 'If I might speak alone with Runcorn for a few minutes . . . ?' he requested. 'Is there somewhere suitable?'

'Oh . . . yes, yes, of course.' Costain rose wearily to his feet. He looked like an old man, confused, stumbling in both mind and body, although he was barely over fifty. 'If you would come this way . . .'

Runcorn excused himself to Naomi, thanking her for her support, nodding to Warner, then he followed Faraday and Costain across the hall to a small study. The fire was only now dying, still offering considerable warmth to the air. Heavy velvet curtains were drawn against the night and the spattering of rain on the glass was almost inaudible here. The walls were lined with bookshelves, but Runcorn had only a moment in which to notice that a large proportion of them were theological, a few on the history or geography of Biblical lands, including Egypt and Mesopotamia.

As soon as the door had closed behind Costain, Faraday turned to Runcorn.

Outside the thunder cracked again.

'I appreciate your help, Runcorn, but let me make this perfectly clear. I will not have you taking over this investigation as if it were some London backstreet. You will not cross-question these good and decent people about their lives as if they were criminals. They are the victims of a hideous tragedy, and deserving of every compassion we can afford them. Do you understand me?' He looked doubtful as if already he was seeking a way to extricate himself from his decision to allow Runcorn to help.

'Even in London people are capable of honour and grief when someone they love is murdered,' Runcorn said hotly, his good intentions swept away by a protective anger for the people he had known, and for all the other victims of loss, whoever they were. The poor did not love any less or have any different protection from pain.

Faraday flushed. 'I apologise,' he said gruffly. 'That was not what I meant to imply. But these people are my respon-sibility. You will be as discreet as you can, and report to me every time you make any discovery that could be relevant to Miss Costain's death. Where do you propose to begin?'

'With the family,' Runcorn replied. 'First I would like to know far more about her than I do. Ugly as it is, she was killed by someone who was standing in front of her, and she was not running from him, which makes it inescapable that she knew him. Had a stranger accosted her alone at night, in the churchyard, she would have run away, or at the very least have fought. She did neither.'

'For God's sake, what are you suggesting?' Faraday said hoarsely. 'That one of her family butchered her? That is unspeakable, and I will not have you—'

'I am stating the facts to you,' Runcorn cut across him. 'Of course I will not put it in those terms to her family. What are you suggesting, sir? That we allow whoever it was to get away with it because looking for him might prove uncomfortable, or embarrassing?'

Faraday was white-faced.

Runcorn had a sudden flash of understanding. 'If you allow me to ask the ugly questions, Sir Alan, it will at least relieve you of the blame for it. You may then be able to be of some comfort to them afterwards.' He did not say that he could blame Runcorn for any offence to their privacy, but the meaning was plain.

Faraday seized it. 'Yes, yes, I suppose that is so. Then you had better proceed. But for heaven's sake, man, be tactful. Use whatever sensitivity you have.'

Runcorn bit back his response. 'Yes, sir,' he said between his teeth. 'I shall begin immediately with Mr Costain, as soon as you have finished speaking with him yourself.'

'For God's sake!' Faraday exploded. 'It's already nearly eight o'clock in the evening. Let the poor man have a little peace. Have you no . . .'

'No time to waste,' Runcorn concluded for him. 'It will be no less powerful tomorrow.'

Faraday gave him a look of intense dislike, but he did not bother to argue any further.

It was no more than a quarter of an hour before the door opened and Costain came in alone.

54

'Please sit down, sir.' Runcorn indicated the armchair opposite the desk.

Costain obeyed. The angle of light from the gaslamp on the wall showed the ravages in his face with peculiar vividness.

'I'm sorry to pursue this, Mr Costain,' Runcorn began, and he meant it honestly. The man's emotions filled the room with turmoil. 'I will make it as brief as I can.'

'Thank you. I would be obliged if you did not have to trouble my wife with this. She and Olivia were . . .' Costain's voice caught and he needed a moment to regain control, '. . . were very close, more like natural sisters, in spite of the difference in their ages,' he finished.

For a moment there was life again in Costain's face as memory flooded back. 'They both loved the island. They would walk for miles, especially in the summer. Take a picnic and spend all day away, when duties allowed. My wife especially was fond of wildflowers. We have many here that one does not find anywhere else. And of course birds. Olivia loved them. She would watch them ride the wind.'

For an intensely vivid moment Runcorn remembered her face as she had passed him in the aisle of the church, and he found it easy to believe her heart had flown with the birds, her imagination far up in the light beyond the reach of earth. No wonder she had been killed with passion. She was the kind of woman who would stir uncontrollable feelings in others: inadequacy, failure, a sense of blindness and frustration, perhaps envy. Not love; love, however unrequited, did not destroy.

Costain had overcome his feelings again, at least enough to continue. 'I cannot see how that is of help to you, Mr Runcorn. Olivia was . . . good-hearted but . . . I regret to say it, undisciplined. She had great compassion – no one was more generous or more diligent in caring for the needy of the parish, whether in goods or in friendship – but she had no true sense of duty.'

Runcorn was confused. 'Duty?' he questioned.

'Of what is appropriate, of what is . . .' Costain hunted for the word. His face showed how acutely aware he was of their social difference and how keen to explain what he meant without being offensive. 'It was already late for her to marry,' he said with a slight flush in his cheeks. 'She refused many perfectly good offers, without reason except her own . . . wilfulness. I had hoped that she would accept Newbridge, but she was reluctant. She wanted something from him quite unrealistic, and I failed to persuade her.' The edge of pain in his voice was like a raw wound. 'I failed her altogether,' he whispered.

'I believe Mr Barclay also courted her?' Runcorn asked, longing to fill the silence with something more than pity.

'Oh, yes. And he would have been an excellent match for her, but she showed no inclination to accept him either.' Costain's shoulders bowed in confusion and defeat.

Runcorn saw Olivia as a beautiful creature refusing to be bound by the walls of convention and other people's perception of her duty. He remembered Melisande standing in the doorway of Barclay's house in London, wanting to help, and Barclay ordering her inside because he was unwilling to become involved in something as ugly as murder. He did not care about the bruising to her conscience. It had probably not even occurred to him. Had he been thinking of her more practical welfare, trying to protect her from dangers she did not see? Or merely protecting himself?

Runcorn saw in Costain, sitting opposite him in the lamplight, still hunched, a man imprisoned in his calling and his social station, bound to duties he had no capacity to meet. Perhaps no one could have. He was too filled with misery to offer Runcorn much more practical help.

'Thank you, sir,' Runcorn said as gently as he could. 'Would you please ask Mrs Costain to spare me a few minutes?'

Costain looked up sharply. 'I asked you not to disturb my wife any further, Mr Runcorn. I thought you understood that?'

'I wish I could oblige you, sir, but I cannot. She may be able to tell me of things Miss Costain confided in her, a quarrel, someone who troubled her or pursued her . . .'

'You are suggesting it was someone my sister knew! That is preposterous.' He stood up.

Runcorn felt brutal. 'It was someone she knew, Mr Costain. The evidence makes that clear.'

'Evidence? Faraday said nothing of that!'

'I will describe it if you wish, but I think it is better if you do not have to hear it.'

Costain closed his eyes and seemed to sway on his feet. Perhaps it was a wavering of the lamplight. 'Please do not tell my wife this.' His voice was no more than a whisper. 'Is this why you think Faraday inadequate to the investigation?'

Runcorn was caught off guard. He had had no idea his opinion was so clear. He certainly had not meant it to be. Should he lie? Costain deserved better, and he had already seen much of the truth.

'Yes, sir.'

'Then do what you have to.' Costain turned and made his way to the door, fumbling with the handle before he could open it.

Naomi Costain came in a few moments later and closed the door behind her before she sat down. Her face was pale, and in the lamplight the stain of recent tears was visible, even though she had done her best to disguise it. There was a kind of hopelessness in her that was more eloquent than all the words of loss she might have spoken.

'I will be as brief as I can, ma'am.' Runcorn felt a deep sense of intrusion.

'There is no need to,' she replied. 'Time is of no importance to me. What can I tell you that would help?'

'Mr Costain said that you and your sister-in-law were very close.' He hated his own words; they sounded so trite. 'If I knew more about her, I might understand the kind of person who would wish her harm.'

She stared into the distance for so long he began to think she was not going to answer, possibly even that she had not understood that it was a question. He drew in his breath to try a different approach when at last she ended the silence.

'She had imagination,' she said slowly, testing each word to be certain it was what she meant. 'She would never be told what to think, and my husband found that . . . wilful, as if she were deliberately disobedient. I don't believe it was. I think it was a kind of honesty. But it made her difficult at times.'

Runcorn knew little of society, especially on an island like this. He needed to understand the jealousies, the ambitions, the feelings that could escalate into the kind of savagery he had seen perpetrated against her.

'Was there anyone she challenged?' he asked, fumbling for a way to ask what he wanted without hurting her even more. 'She was beautiful. Were there men who admired her, women who were rivals?'

Naomi smiled. 'You knew her?'

He felt as if some opportunity had passed him by. 'No. I saw her once, in church.'

The smile faded.

'Oh. Yes, of course. I expect people were envious. It happens, especially against those who do not conform to the way of life expected of them. She did not have many friends.

She grew very impatient sometimes. It is not a good quality. I used to hope she would learn to curb it, in time.' She sighed. 'She liked Mrs Ewart. At first I thought it was just because she was from London, and brought a touch of glamour with her. She could speak of the latest plays and books, music, and that sort of thing. But then I saw it was deeper than that. They understood something that I did not.' A sadness filled her face again, a kind of loneliness that Runcorn found to his amazement that he understood. It was a knowledge of exclusion, as if someone had gone, and left them alone in the dark.

'Was she happy?' he asked impulsively.

Naomi looked at him with surprise. 'No.' Then instantly she regretted it. 'I mean that she was restless, she was looking for something. I . . . no, really, please disregard me, I am talking nonsense. I have no idea who could have been so deranged by envy or fear as to have done such a thing.'

Runcorn had the overpowering feeling that she was lying – not perhaps in literal words but certainly in meaning. She knew something she was not prepared to tell him. 'The best thing you can do for her, Mrs Costain, is to help us find who killed her,' he said urgently.

She rose to her feet, her face weary, her eyes very direct. 'Do you believe that, Mr Runcorn? How little you know us, or perhaps anyone. You are a good man, but you do not know the wind or the waves of the heart. Landlocked,' she added, walking to the door. 'You are all landlocked.'

60

It was too late for Runcorn to see anyone else that night, and his mind was in too much confusion of feeling and impression to absorb any more. He thanked Costain, and went out into the darkness to walk back to Mrs Owen's lodging house. The rain had stopped and the wind was bitter, but he was thankful to be alive. He liked the clean smell of the sea, wild as it was, and the absence of human sounds. There were no voices, no clip of horses' hoofs, no rattle of wheels, only the hoot of a tawny owl.

It was difficult to gain an interview with Newbridge and it took Runcorn the best part of the morning before he finally stood face to face with him in his withdrawing room. The house was old and comfortable. Possibly it had stood in those grounds for two centuries or more, occupied by the one family in times both fat and lean. There were portraits on the walls that bore the same cast of features back to the time of the Civil War. They were dressed in the ruffles and lace of the Cavaliers. There were no grim-faced, white-collared Puritans.

Some of the furniture had been magnificent in its time, but it now bore marks of heavy use. Legs were uneven, one or two surfaces were stained and needed repolishing. Runcorn had time to notice no more than that before he was aware of Newbridge's impatience.

'What is it you want, Mr Runcorn?' There was a thickness to his voice and he moved his weight from one foot to the other as though he were anxious to be elsewhere. 'I have nothing I can tell you about poor Olivia's death. If I had, I would have told Faraday, for God's sake! Is it not bad enough that we have to live with this tragedy without having to drag out all our memories and our grief over and over again for strangers?'

He stood leaning against the mantelshelf, an elegant man, tall and a little lean, with wavy hair that grew high from his forehead. His eyes were hazel, deep set, and there was a thin, angry line to his mouth.

Runcorn found his tolerance already stretched. Loss had different effects on people, and in many it was not attractive. In men it often turned to anger, a kind of suppressed fury that they had been dealt a blow.

Runcorn bit back his own emotions. 'In order to have some better idea of who might have killed her, sir, I need to know more about her. Her family are overweighed with grief just now, and of course they see only one side of her. It is very difficult to speak anything but good of the dead you have loved, and yet they were also human, like the rest of us. She was not killed by accident. Someone was consumed by an unholy rage, and stood face to face with her, and even at the last moment, she did not run away. That needs explaining.'

Newbridge was very pale and his chest rising and falling as if he had climbed to a great altitude and was struggling for breath.

'Are you saying that something in her nature provoked the act, Mr Runcorn?' he said at last.

'Do you think that impossible?' Runcorn kept his voice low, as though they were confiding in each other.

'Well ... it's ... you place me in a terrible situation,' Newbridge protested. 'How can I observe any decency, and answer such a question?'

'There was no decency in the way she was killed, or indeed that she was killed at all,' Runcorn pointed out.

Newbridge sighed. His face was even paler. 'Then you force me in honour to speak more frankly than I would have wished. But if you repeat it to her family I shall deny it.'

Runcorn nodded very slightly.

'She was charming,' Newbridge said, looking somewhere away from Runcorn into a distance only he could see. 'And beautiful, but I imagine you know that. She was also childish. She was twenty-six, an age when most women are married and have children, and yet she refused to grow up.' His body stiffened. 'She would not take any responsibility for herself, which placed an unfair burden upon her brother. I think she took advantage of the fact that he is childless to remain immature herself, and charge him with her care long past the time when she should have accepted that burden herself.'

'Do you think Mr Costain resented this?'

'He is too good a man to have refused to care for her,' Newbridge answered. 'And frankly I think he indulged her. His sense of obligation as a clergyman was out of proportion. She knew that and took advantage of it.'

That was the harshest thing Runcorn had heard said of

Olivia, and he was startled how it hurt him. For all he knew, it might be true, but he was smarting as if it had been Melisande of whom it had been said. And yet he could think of no reply. He kept his own emotion tightly in check, unaware that he was clenching his muscles and that his nails dug into the palms of his hands.

'Indeed?' He said the word between his teeth. 'Did she make use of anyone else's goodwill in such a way?'

The silence weighed heavily for several moments. Somewhere outside a dog barked, and a gust of rain beat against the windows. The urgency of it brought Newbridge back to the present as if some reverie had been broken. An anger within him came under control, or perhaps it was grief. Runcorn found it impossible to tell, no matter how carefully he watched. He felt intrusive. This man had wanted to marry Olivia. How hard it must be for him to govern his emotions in front of an inquisitive stranger who had seen her hideously dead, but never known or loved her alive.

'She did not, so far as I am aware,' Newbridge said finally. 'Mrs Costain was very fond of her, and she had other friends as well. Mrs Ewart. And Mr Barclay was courting her. But I imagine you know that. She was friendly with the curate, Kelsall, and various young women in the town, at least in a casual way. Most of them were married, of course, and not free to waste their time in pursuit of dreams, as she did.' He looked away from Runcorn again, as if trying to imagine he was not there. 'Or to spend hours reading,' he went on. 'They may have met in charitable work. She was always willing to help those less fortunate, whether they were deserving or not. There was a generosity in her—' He stopped abruptly, his head still turned. 'Look, I really cannot help you. I have no idea who would want to hurt her, or why. The only possible suggestion I can make is to look more closely at John Barclay. He came to the island only lately. He's a Londoner. Perhaps he lost patience with her indecision. On the other hand, perhaps I merely dislike the man.' He faced Runcorn at last. 'Now, if you will excuse me, I have nothing further to add. My butler will show you to the door.'

Runcorn had no choice but to see Barclay next. It was an interview he was not looking forward to but it was unavoidable. Was it really possible that he had lost his temper with Olivia, and faced her in the churchyard with a carving knife? Runcorn disliked the man, but he found that difficult to believe of him. A hot temper to say something in spite he did not doubt for a moment, even a physical blow to another man, but premeditated murder of such bloody violence was outside Runcorn's imagination of him.

Nevertheless as he walked up the driveway of the great house, sheltered by laurels, his feet crunching on the gravel, he felt a distinct flutter of fear in the pit of his stomach. He did not imagine for an instant that Barclay would attack him, but even if he did, Runcorn had never been a physical coward. He was tall and powerful, and had fought many battles in the

streets of the East End in his earlier years. It was the ugliness of misery and hate that frightened him, the brutality of
Melisande learning that her brother was capable of such acts,
and would have to face the public shame of it. The scandal
would follow her as long as she lived, not from any guilt of
hers, but by association.

But if Runcorn were to evade the interview now, even for
her sake, then he betrayed himself, and the principles he
believed in and had sworn an oath to uphold. He was a servant
of the law and the people, and at the moment, as he stood
on the front step of this beautiful house on the Isle of Anglesey,
as if it were a crossroads in the journey of his mind, that was
more important than pleasing anyone else. If he forswore his
duty then after he had parted from Melisande and left Anglesey
he would have nothing left.

The butler answered the door and, to Runcorn's surprise,
invited him to go into the morning room, and he would inform
Mr Barclay of his presence.

Runcorn accepted and followed the man's stiff figure across
the parquet floor to the faded, comfortable room facing on
to the side garden. A fire was lit and several armchairs were
pulled into a ring around it. Two bookcases were filled with
volumes that had the look of use. A bowl of holly leaves and
berries sat on a low table. Runcorn knew it was a house taken
only for the season, but it had an air of being lived in with
ease and a certain familiarity.

Barclay appeared after nearly a quarter of an hour, but he

seemed in an agreeable mood and made no objection to Runcorn having called without prior appointment.

'Learn anything yet?' he asked conversationally, coming in and closing the door.

Runcorn found himself relaxing a fraction. He realised Melisande must have prepared the way for him, at least as much as she could. He should respond with tact, for her sake.

'It appears that Miss Costain was a more complex person than we had at first assumed,' he replied.

Barclay shrugged. 'One always wishes to speak well of the dead, particularly when they have died violently, and young. It's a natural kind of decency, almost like laying flowers.' He did not sit, or invite Runcorn to, so they both remained standing at opposite sides of the fire.

It was Runcorn's turn to speak. He tried to frame his questions as if he were asking for assistance. 'I am trying to find out as much as I can where everyone was leading up to the time Miss Costain was killed. Something must have caused it to happen . . .'

Barclay's face registered a quick understanding. 'You mean a quarrel or a discovery, that kind of thing?'

'Exactly.' Runcorn was glad to be able to agree. 'Sergeant Warner has already done a great deal in that line, but I was wondering if you could help any further. You knew Miss Costain. Were you aware of any events that day, anyone she saw, or who was angry or distressed with her?'

He was not sure what he expected. For the time being,

simply to talk was good. He could move slowly from small facts to larger passions.

Barclay gave it some thought. 'She could be a difficult woman,' he said after a while. 'A dreamer rather than a realist, if you know what I mean?' He met Runcorn's eyes. 'Some women are a trifle impractical, especially if they have always been cared for by a father or elder brother, and never had to consider the real world. Olivia . . . Olivia was spoiled. She was charming and generous. She could be an excellent companion. But there was in her a streak of wilfulness, a clinging on to childhood dreams and fancies which could become tedious after a while. I felt for Costain.' He gave a slight shrug, as if confiding an understanding better implied than spoken.

'Did they quarrel?' Runcorn asked.

'Oh, for heaven's sake, not to the point where he would take a knife and follow her up to the graveyard and kill her!' Barclay looked appalled. 'But I'm sure she tested his patience sorely. It is not an easy thing to be responsible for one's sister. You have a father's distress and obligation without a father's authority.' He spread his hands in a gesture of futility. 'I don't doubt for an instant that he did the best he could, but she was flighty, unrealistic, apparently unaware of her own responsibilities in return.'

He gave a slight smile. 'Made me grateful that my own sister is so much more sensible. Faraday will make an excellent husband for her. He has every quality one could desire.

He is of fine family; he can provide for her both financially and socially. He is of spotless reputation, good temperament, altogether a thoroughly decent fellow. And fine-looking as well, which is hardly necessary, but it is very agreeable. Melisande is a beautiful woman, and could take her pick from quite a few. I'm most grateful that she has more good sense than Olivia had, and does not entertain absurd fancies.' He held Runcorn's eyes and smiled steadily and coldly.

Runcorn's head was crowded with an avalanche of thoughts and feelings, bruising him, crushing sense and rational meaning. He struggled to think of something to say that was sensible, purely practical, and would remove that smirk from Barclay's lips.

'You are right.' The words were thick and clumsy on his tongue. 'A sane man does not murder his sister because she is disinclined to marry the suitor he has chosen for her. Or are you suggesting that Costain may not be sane?'

Barclay's smile vanished. 'No, of course not. I meant only that Olivia could at times try the patience of even a good man. If there were a man less devoted to decency, less governed by the affections of a brother and more of a lover, or would-be lover, then he might be less . . . sane.' He lifted his shoulders very slightly. 'Someone killed her. Thank God it is not my trade, or my duty to find out who. I cannot think of anything more unsavoury than hunting through the sins and griefs of other people's lives in search of the final depravity, but I appreciate that someone has to do it, if we are to have the rule of law. If I can be of assistance to you, then naturally I shall do what I can.'

'Thank you,' Runcorn said bleakly.

Barclay dismissed the reply with a gesture of his hand, and before Runcorn could frame the next question he continued, 'I would be obliged if you did not harass my sister with this any more than is absolutely necessary. She was fond of Miss Costain. They had certain situations in life in common, and Melisande is a soft-hearted woman, at times a trifle naïve. She was inclined to believe whatever Olivia told her, and I fear it was not always the truth. She was not a good influence.' His smile returned.

'I am glad that Melisande is committed to Faraday, and will soon be settled. Perhaps she would have been able to prevail upon Olivia, had she lived. But that is tragically of no importance any more. If I can think further, I shall certainly inform you.' He turned the corners of his mouth down. 'Unpleasant word, "inform". Sounds as if it were clandestine, somehow deceitful, but then to defend someone guilty of such a crime would be even worse, wouldn't it?' It was half a question, the answer assumed.

Runcorn found the words sticking in his throat, but he had to force himself to agree. 'Yes, sir, I regret that murder frequently exposes many smaller sins that can change the quality of our lives for ever afterwards.'

Barclay stared at him, an expression in his eyes that was

impossible to read: anger, triumph, a knowledge of his own power, an uncertainty.

'Thank you, Mr Barclay,' Runcorn said quietly. 'I appreciate your assistance. I wish everyone were as honourable in their duty.'

If Barclay detected any sarcasm, he did not show it even by a flicker.

The curate, Kelsall, was utterly different from Barclay. Runcorn caught up with him as he strode doggedly through the pounding rain on his visits to the parish's old and needy. Some of them would normally be Costain's duty, but in the circumstances Kelsall had taken it upon himself.

'You may think it arrogant of me,' he said to Runcorn as they kept pace with each other. 'Some people might prefer to see the vicar himself, but just now not only is he spending time with poor Mrs Costain, but he does not know how to answer people. What can they say to him? That they are sorry? She was the most charming, the most vividly alive person they ever knew, and her death is like God taking some of the light from the world?' He kept his face resolutely forward. 'And what can he say, except agree, and try to keep from embarrassing them with his pain? It is better I go. At least they do not feel as if they have to sympathise with me the same. I can address their problems, which is what I am there for.'

'But you did know her well, and feel her death very hard.'

71

Runcorn knew it was brutal, but stretching it out with euphemisms would be like pulling a plaster off slowly. And it was less honest.

'We were friends,' Kelsall replied simply. 'We could speak to each other about all manner of things without having to pretend we felt differently. If something was funny we laughed, even if sometimes people thought it was inappropriate. Our eyes would meet and we would each know the other thought the same. We both understood what it was to have dreams . . . and regrets.' His voice trembled a little. 'I cannot imagine I will ever like anyone else quite so much, so fully.'

Runcorn looked sideways at him, plunging forward into the wind and rain, and did not know for certain whether it was tears that wet his cheeks or the weather. He believed, and even hoped, that it was the former.

They reached the house of one elderly parishioner, and Runcorn waited outside, shivering in the lee of the porch, until Kelsall returned. They set out walking again.

'Is it true that Miss Costain refused Mr Newbridge's offer of marriage?' Runcorn asked after forty or fifty paces.

Kelsall hunched his shoulders and walked more intently forward. Thunder rumbled around the horizon. 'She was a woman of deep feelings,' he said, shaking his head a little and fumbling for the right words. 'Visionary. You could never have tied her down to petty things. It would have broken her. He couldn't see that. He didn't love her, he liked what he thought she was and did not look closely enough to see that he was utterly wrong. I don't think he even . . . listened.' He looked suddenly at Runcorn. 'Why do people marry someone they don't even listen to? How can they bear to be so lonely?' He was shuddering, waving his hands as he strode. 'Of course she refused him. What else could she do?'

Runcorn did not reply, in his mind for a moment he saw the face of the girl in green as she had passed him in church. Then he saw Melisande, and the bland, handsome features of Faraday, and he was filled with the same helpless despair as he heard in Kelsall. Had he loved Olivia? Would their relationship have been infinitely more than friendship if he could have chosen? Was there a completely different kind of hunger beneath the grief he displayed in his young, vulnerable face? Runcorn did not think so.

They walked together without speaking again, and he left Kelsall at his next parishioner's house.

Making his way back up the incline again to find Warner, Runcorn did not change his mind. He still thought Kelsall a friend, but perhaps a closer one, more observant, more of a confidant than he had at first assumed.

The redwings were gone from the field. He hoped they would be back after the rain.

He spent the afternoon with Warner but the only thing that emerged from their efforts was that Kelsall was accounted for by an absent-minded old gentleman he had been visiting and who had at last remembered what had happened on which evening.

In the late afternoon, just before dusk, there was a sudden lifting of the clouds and the air was filled with the soft, warm light of the fading sun, already touching the high ground with a patina of gold. Suddenly the sea was blue and the Menai Strait a shining mirror barely wind-rippled as the icy breath of the sky whispered across it and disappeared.

Runcorn started to walk again, drawn towards the shore. It was cold, but he did not mind. There was a sweetness to the coast, a width that strangely excited him.

He stood and craned his neck upwards as he watched gulls soaring on the invisible currents, careening sideways and slipping down and then up, looking effortless as they mounted into the light and were lost to view.

It was almost silent, a faint whisper of water behind him. London had never offered him such infinite peace. There was always noise, some kind of clatter of human occupation, an end to vision, to possibility.

He went on climbing upward. Perhaps he was wrong, and he had allowed himself to believe in limits where there were none, except those he made for himself. He thought of the past with a different view, almost as if he were regarding someone else. He saw a man of practical common sense, judgement of character that was usually right, but without empathy. He lacked a passion, an understanding of dreams. Had he guarded himself from such things, afraid to face his own smallness? He had hated Monk's anger and his fire, his impatience with stupidity, his arrogance. Or more truly was he afraid of it, because it challenged the conformity that was so much less dangerous?

Was that what Olivia had done too, challenged conformity? She had climbed these hills – he knew that from Naomi Costain. She might even have stood on this level stretch of the path and stared at the fire of the setting sun, as he was doing, and looked at the horizon where the sky and the sea became one.

Small people who want to be safe, who have no driving hunger, are afraid of those who upset their world, remove the boundaries that close them in and excuse their cowardice. He had hated Monk for that. Who had hated Olivia? Not Naomi. But what about Costain? Did she question this edifice of his faith, the daily justification of his status, his income, his reason for being? Could he forgive her that?

Or was he simply a good man who did not understand a difficult sister whom it was his responsibility to feed and clothe, and keep within society's bounds, for her own sake?

The sun was a scarlet ball on the horizon, and even as Runcorn watched, it dropped below the rim, spilling fire across the sea. He would stand here as darkness gathered and closed in, wondering what Olivia had felt. What visions had she seen, and perhaps died for? Was Melisande anything like her, except in his imagination? But he was a practical man, trained by years of making himself fit the mould of necessity, and the only real service he could perform now was to discover the truth. It might help no one to name the guilty, but it was surely a necessary service to free the innocent from blame, others' and their own.

In the morning Runcorn rose early and ate the rich breakfast Mrs Owen cooked for him. She seemed to enjoy filling the plate to overflowing with bacon, eggs and potato cakes, then watching him make his way through it. He did not really want so much, and initially he ate it only to satisfy her sense of hospitality. But in succeeding days he had talked with her and learned with growing interest her opinions of various people in the village, and involved in the case. Her perception was homely, but sometimes surprisingly acute.

'Just the right man for the vicarage here, Mr Costain is,' she said. 'Poor soul, his wife. Lonely, I think. No children. Doesn't know how to talk without really saying anything, if you know what I mean? People don't always want to think. Like Miss Olivia, she was.'

Runcorn had his mouth full and was unable to ask her to explain further, and he was not certain that if he did, then she would not think that perhaps she had said too much, and be far more discreet in future.

'Like some more tea, Mr Runcorn?' she offered, the pot in her hand. 'Helps a lot of things, from a headache to a broken heart. Lovely girl, Miss Olivia was. Quick to sorrow, and quick to joy, God rest her. Never found anyone for herself, that I know of, in spite of what they said.'

Runcorn swallowed his mouthful whole and nearly choked

himself. 'What did they say?' he asked huskily, reaching for the tea to wash it down.

'Just silly gossip,' she replied. 'Nothing to it. Would you like another piece of toast, Mr Runcorn?'

He declined, finished his tea, and set out to look for Kelsall. This time he found him in the church and he stopped his tidying and general preparation as soon as he saw Runcorn walking up the aisle.

'Do you know something?' he asked, striding towards him, black cassock swinging.

Runcorn felt a twinge of failure, as if he should have done better. 'Not yet.'

'Perhaps if we leave, we will not be interrupted,' Kelsall suggested. 'Here I am always "on duty", as it were. It's cold outside, but at the moment it's not raining.' He suited his actions to the words without waiting to see if Runcorn agreed. In the graveyard he matched his steps to Runcorn's and at the same time managed to guide their way out of the gate and on to a road leading out of the village towards the open hillside.

'Why do people kill others, Mr Runcorn?' he asked. 'I have been thinking of it all night. If any man knows, it is surely you. It is such a . . . a barbarous and futile way to solve anything.'

Runcorn looked at his earnest face and knew that the question was perfectly serious. Perhaps it was one he should have asked himself in more detail days ago.

'Several reasons,' he said thoughtfully. 'Sometimes it is greed, for money, for power, for property such as a house. Sometimes for something as trivial as an ornament or a piece of jewellery.'

'Not Olivia,' Kelsall said with certainty. 'She had no possessions of any note. She was entirely dependent on her brother.'

'Ambition,' Runcorn continued. 'It can drive people to violence, or betrayal.'

'Olivia's death helps no one,' Kelsall responded. 'Anyway, there is nothing around here to aspire to. It is all predictable, small offices, of no great power.'

Runcorn turned over all the past cases he could think of, coming at last to those of passion, such as to cause the terrible wound he had seen in Olivia's body. 'Jealousy,' he said grimly. 'She was beautiful, and from what people say, she had a quality unlike anyone else, a fire and a courage different from others of her age and position. That can also make people feel uncomfortable, even threatened. People can kill out of fear.'

For about fifty paces Kelsall did not respond 'What kind of fear?' he said at length.

Runcorn heard the change in his voice and knew that suddenly they were treading delicately, on the edge of truth. He must act slowly; he might be about to rip the veil from a pain that had not been seen naked from lies before.

'All kinds,' he said, watching Kelsall's face, profile towards him, his eyes and the lines of his mouth half hidden.

'Sometimes it is of physical pain, but more often it is fear of loss.'

'Loss . . .' Kelsall tasted the word carefully. 'What sort of loss?'

Runcorn did not answer, hoping Kelsall would suggest something himself.

They walked another fifty paces. The wind was easing off, although the clouds were low and dark to the east.

'You mean fear of scandal?' Kelsall asked. 'Or ridicule?'

'Certainly. Many victims of blackmail have killed their tormentors.' Was this what had happened? Olivia had learned a secret that somebody was afraid she would use? He looked as closely as he dared, but he could see no change in Kelsall's expression. He still looked hurt and confused.

There was no sound but the wind in the grass, and far away the echo of waves breaking on the rocks.

'Olivia wasn't like that,' Kelsall said finally. 'She would never repeat anyone's secrets, still less would she use them. What for? The things she wanted could not be bought.'

'What did she want?'

'Freedom,' he said without hesitation. 'She wanted to be herself, not the person convention said she should be. Perhaps we all want it, or think we do, but few of us are prepared to pay the price. It hurts to be different.' He stopped and faced Runcorn. 'Is that why she was murdered, because she made other people aware of how ordinary they were, how easily they denied their dreams?'

'I doubt it,' Runcorn said gently. 'Wouldn't someone who was able to see that in her also know that killing her would make no difference whatever to their own . . . futility?'

'Not if she laughed at them,' Kelsall replied. 'Some people cannot bear to be mocked. Ridicule can hurt beyond some people's power to bear, Mr Runcorn. It strikes the very core of who you believe yourself to be. One can forgive many things, but not being made to see yourself as ridiculous, a coward at life. That kind of rage is acid in the soul.'

Was he speaking of himself? Runcorn wondered for a moment of horror and acute misery if he was on the brink of hearing a confession. It would hurt. He genuinely liked the young man. He had seen his gentleness with the frail and old, the lasting sense of their dignity kept, help given as a privilege, not a duty.

'What do you know, Mr Kelsall?' he asked. 'I think it is time you spoke the truth.'

'I know that Newbridge and Barclay were at daggers drawn over Olivia, but I don't know if either of them really even wanted her, or simply hated each other because the battle was public. Some people do not take to losing with grace.'

Runcorn struggled to follow. 'If that were so, would they not kill each other, rather than her?'

Kelsall shrugged, and started walking again. 'I suppose so. Or even Faraday. Although it's a bit late for that now.'

'The chief constable?' Runcorn caught up with him. 'What has he to do with it?'

'Oh, he courted her too, a while ago,' Kelsall replied. 'The poor vicar thought that would have been an excellent match, even though Faraday was quite a few years older than she. He thought it would settle her down a bit. But she gave him no encouragement at all, and he soon grew tired of it.'

'Faraday?' The name burst from Runcorn in amazement, and a kind of dull and momentary anger. He had courted Olivia, and now he was going to marry Melisande. There was no place for reason in his reaction, no small, sane voice telling him most men did not marry their first love, or even their second. Olivia had refused him. And Melisande had been obliged to accept him.

He was being ridiculous, he knew it, and still his thoughts raced on. Faraday might have lost interest in Olivia because she was flighty, a dreamer, irresponsible. He might love Melisande because she was gentler, a visionary still capable of loving the real, the human and fallible. A woman not only beautiful but brave enough to accept an ordinary man, and perhaps in time make of him something greater.

Kelsall was still talking but Runcorn had not listened. He had to ask him to repeat it, and drag his attention back to the one thing he was good at, the skill that gave him his identity.

'You said something about Mr Barclay?' he prompted.

Kelsall shook his head a little. 'I think the vicar envies him,' he repeated.

'Why?' Although Runcorn feared that he knew the answer.

81

Kelsall smiled without pleasure. 'His sister did not argue with him. He had a way of making her understand what had to be done, what life requires of us, if we are to survive. I think he would have persuaded Olivia as well, only he stopped wishing to, just before she died. I have no idea why, or I would have told you. The vicar thought Barclay a fine match for her. Only Mrs Costain did not care for him.' He gave a slight shrug. 'But then she did not care for Newbridge either, so far as I could see. The vicar accused her of wishing Olivia to remain single because she was such a good companion. But of course it was no good for her. She should marry and have her own home, and children, like any other woman. And to be honest, it is something of an expense on a clergyman's stipend to dress and provide for two women.' He looked deeply unhappy. 'Fear of poverty is not the same thing as greed, Mr Runcorn. Really it is not.'

'No,' Runcorn said quietly. 'No, it is a very human and natural thing. Perhaps Miss Costain was not aware of the drain she was on his resources.'

'No. I think she was not always very practical,' Kelsall conceded. 'It takes a long time for a man of the cloth to earn enough to keep a wife, never mind a sister as well.' There was loneliness and self-mockery in his voice, and he did not meet Runcorn's eyes.

'Or a policeman,' Runcorn responded. 'But then a policeman's wife would expect far less.' There was self-mockery in his words too. On his salary he could not keep a woman like Melisande for a month, let alone a lifetime. It was not only social class that divided them, or experience and beliefs, it was money and all it could buy, the comforts a woman of Melisande's background would accept without even noticing them.

Kelsall caught the emotion in him, even a shadow of the pain, and looked at him with new intensity, and a sudden flame of gentleness in his eyes. He was tactful enough to say nothing.

Runcorn reported to Faraday as he had been commanded to do. It was an uncomfortable interview, and largely fruitless. He was leaving the vicarage and walking across the church-yard when Melisande caught up with him. She had come out of the house hastily and had no cloak with her. The wind blew her hair off her face and whipped long strands of it out of its pins. It looked soft, giving her a dark, wild halo and showing the pallor of her skin. She was frightened, he could see it in her eyes, but he did not know if it was for herself, or for the ugly things she knew were coming unravelled from people's secrets, pulled at by the fingers of violent death.

He longed to able to comfort her, and found himself word-less, standing there among the grass in the wind.

'Mr Runcorn,' she said urgently, 'forgive me for following you, but I wished so much to speak with you without my brother knowing. Might we go into the lee of the church?

'Of course.' He wondered whether to offer her his arm

over the uneven ground. He would like to feel her touch, even through the thickness of his jacket. He could imagine it. But what if she refused? She might think it was impertinent, a familiarity because she had asked for his help. It was asking for humiliation to assume more, even for an instant. He kept his arm by his side and walked stiffly over to the shelter of the church walls.

The silence was painful and he started to speak as soon as they were there.

'I am learning a great deal more about Miss Costain.' He told her most of what Kelsall had said, but more gently phrased, and he did not mention that Faraday had courted her too, although he wondered if perhaps she knew. 'It seems she was unwilling to accept any marriage her brother recommended for her,' he finished. 'And it was causing some ill feeling, and a degree of financial stress.'

'You mean Mr Newbridge?' Melisande said quickly.

Runcorn did not know how to answer. He had been clumsy. In trying to tell her something of meaning he had put himself in a position where either he had to lie, or admit that it also meant her brother, and her own suitor.

Too quickly she understood. Her smile was self-mocking. 'And John,' she added. 'It is no secret that he courted her as well, although I think he became a little disillusioned with her some short time before her death. I think he requires in a woman more sense of the practical than she was willing to give.' She looked away from him and sighed in exasperation.

'I'm sorry, that is such a foolish euphemism. Olivia was individual. She had the courage at least to attempt to live her dreams. They were not so very unreasonable. She wanted to travel, but she would have worked to achieve that. Of course a vicar's sister is not supposed to work at anything. What is there that a respectable woman can do?' There was an ache of longing in her voice, as if she were speaking of herself, not a friend she understood too well.

'She had no real skills, and not a great deal of practical knowledge of the world,' she continued. 'One cannot survive without at least some money. If one had been born poor one might at least have learned to do something useful. Sometimes I wonder if necessity might not be a better spur than dreams, don't you think?' Without warning she turned to look at him, meeting his eyes with fierce candour. 'Do you like what you do, Mr Runcorn?'

He was at a loss to answer her. He could feel his face flaming, as if she would see his emotions drowning him. 'I . . . not always. I . . . it . . .' This was his one chance to be honest with her. 'Sometimes it is terrible, painful. You see awful things, and cannot help.'

'Isn't that better than seeing nothing at all?' she demanded. 'And at least you can try!'

She was so vivid he almost felt as if he were touching her in the sharp air. The words came easily.

'Yes. And at times I succeed. I can't bring back the dead, and catching the guilty doesn't always make sense, or justice,

85

but it explains. Understanding gets rid of the sense of confusion, the helplessness to know what happened and why.'

She smiled. 'You are fortunate. You have something worth doing. Even if you don't always manage to complete it, at least you know you have tried.'

He had never thought of it like that. Barclay had said he cleared up the detritus of other people's crimes and follies, a sort of sweeper up of dirt. 'Is that how you see it?' he asked uncertainly.

She shook her head. 'Oh, don't think of John. Sometimes he takes pleasure in being offensive. He denigrates what he doesn't understand. It's a kind of . . . fear. We are all afraid of something, if we are honest.'

'What was Olivia afraid of?' He hardly dared ask. Were they speaking of Olivia, or of Melisande herself?

She looked away again. 'Of loneliness,' she answered. 'Of failure. Of coming to the end of one's life and realising all the passionate, beautiful things you could at least have tried to do, but you didn't have the courage. And then it's too late . . .' She stopped, not as if she had no further thought, but as if she could not bear to speak it aloud.

Perhaps he should have turned to the stark outline of the church, or even to the carved and ornamental gravestones beyond, but he did not. The grief in her filled him, and he knew it was not only a compassion for Olivia and the darkness she had felt closing in front of her, but that it was so acute because she could see herself in it and dread the same emptiness. He had never so intensely wanted to touch anyone, but he knew he could not, not even the cold, ungloved hand at her side. There was no comfort he could offer except his skill, and now he was increasingly afraid that what he might learn further of Barclay would prove uglier than she had imagined, and inescapable.

But he too had to follow the truth, wherever it led. This wide, clean land, with its endless distances, had awoken a disturbing awareness in him of his own cramped beliefs in the past, the narrowness that Monk had so despised. Suddenly he wanted to change, for himself, not even for dreams of Melisande, however sweet or hopeless. He was aware of an enormity inside him, of a loss he could feel but not name. The silence of the air was a balm, but something inside him ached to be filled.

'I'll find him,' he said to her. 'But it will not be comfortable. It will show hatred you do not know is here, and weakness you have not had to look at before. I'm sorry.'

'I know,' she accepted. 'It is foolish, like a small child, to imagine that what is behind this dreadful crime is something out there, a piece of madness that just happened to strike us. It comes from inside. Thank you for being so honest.' She hesitated a moment as if to add something else, then simply said good night and, with a brief smile, was gone.

Runcorn took a step after her, not knowing if he should walk beside her back at least to the gate of the big house, then he realised the foolishness of that. She had sought him in the tumble of gravestones, and then the lee of the church, precisely not to be seen.

He turned and made his way back to Mrs Owen, and something hot to eat and drink.

In the morning he reported again to Faraday.

Faraday received him with a flare of hope that he had at last found some concrete evidence, but it died as soon as he saw Runcorn's face.

'I think you misunderstood me, Runcorn,' he said tartly. 'There really is no need to keep coming here to tell me that you have learned nothing.'

Runcorn felt the chill and for an instant the temper he would have exhibited a year ago was hot inside him. He choked it down.

'I had a long talk with Kelsall, sir, and he clarified a great many things in my mind.'

Faraday gave him a sour look of disbelief, but he did not interrupt. His expression said vividly what he considered Runcorn's mind to be worth, if the curate could improve it.

Runcorn felt himself colouring. He knew his voice was tart, but to moderate it was beyond his control. 'He asked the nature of motives for murder. They are generally simple: greed, fear, ambition, revenge, outrage . . .'

'Get to your point, Runcorn. What does that tell us that we did not already know? She was hardly a threat to anyone.'

'Not physically, sir, in reputation or belief, in challenge to authority, in threat to expose what is private, shameful, or embarrassing,' Runcorn explained.

'Oh. You think perhaps Miss Costain was privy to someone's secrets? She would not have betrayed such a thing. If you had known her, you would not even suggest it.'

'Not even if it were illegal?'

Faraday frowned. Suddenly understanding filled his eyes. 'Who? Whose secrets would she know? I shall have to ask Costain.'

'No, sir!'

'Surely he is the most likely to know who— Good God!' Faraday's eyes widened. 'You don't think he—'

'I don't know,' Runcorn cut across him. 'But that is not the only kind of fear. There is the dread of humiliation, of being mocked, of having one's inadequacies laid bare.'

'That seems a bit fanciful,' Faraday said, but the colour in his cheeks belied his words.

'Newbridge courted her and she rejected him,' Runcorn observed, making it a statement. 'So, apparently, did John Barclay.'

Faraday chewed his lips. 'Do you think he is capable of such violence?'

'Did she reject him also?' Runcorn continued.

'Yes, I believe so. Surely he couldn't . . .' His eyes widened again, the question already answered in his mind.

Runcorn saw it and anger burned up inside him for Melisande. This man was going to marry her, and yet in order to solve a murder he was willing to believe that her brother could be guilty. Or was that belief formed from a closer knowledge of him than Runcorn had, especially during the time of his acquaintance with Olivia? Was he finally facing a grief he had tried to avoid, but could not any longer?

'You know him better than I do,' Runcorn said with a greater gentleness. 'How did he accept her rejection? Did he love her deeply?'

Faraday looked startled.

It raced through Runcorn's mind that what he dreamed of as love was not something Faraday even considered. There was no understanding of the passion, the hunger, the tenderness, the soaring of the heart or the plunge of despair. He was thinking of an arrangement, an affection. Runcorn was harrowed up with a rage so intense he could have struck Faraday's smug, bland face and beaten his assumptions out of him. He wanted to feel blood and bone under his fists.

Was that what had happened to someone with Olivia, only they had used as carving knife? Why? Could the murderer have been a woman, someone with no physical ability to strike, but the passion nevertheless?

'It doesn't have to be a man,' he said aloud. 'Who else did Newbridge court? Or John Barclay? Who could have loved or wanted them with such fierce possessiveness?'

'A woman?' Faraday was stunned. 'But it was . . . violent! Brutal.'

'Women can be just as brutal as men,' Runcorn said tartly.

'It happens less often, simply for opportunity and perhaps schooling, but the rage is just as savage, and when it breaks through the years of self-control, it will be uglier.'

'Jealousy?' Faraday tasted the idea. Now he was meeting Runcorn's eyes and there was no evasion in him, no weariness. 'Over Newbridge? I don't think so. Although to be honest, I hadn't considered it. I'll have Warner look into it more closely. John Barclay, that seems possible. He can be very charming, and he has a high opinion of himself. He would not take rejection easily. Neither he nor Newbridge.'

He shrugged with a slight smile 'She was a difficult young woman, Runcorn. If you intend to solve her murder, you must recognise that. She was a dreamer, impractical, selfish, very wilful in certain matters. She steadily refused to be guided by her brother, a patient and long-suffering man, where she was concerned and, I regret to say, not always best supported by his wife. John Barclay is much more fortunate, and I dare say wiser, even if he has a certain vanity.'

Runcorn felt the iron vice closing around Melisande as if around himself. In his mind he stood with her again in the churchyard and heard her speaking of Olivia, the emotion trembling in her voice, and he knew it was also for herself. But she obeyed necessity, understanding there was no choice. Olivia had rebelled. Were they connected? How? There was still no pattern he could read to throw light on anyone's innocence or guilt.

'Thank you,' Faraday said briskly, cutting across his

thoughts. 'The fact that it might have been a woman would explain why Miss Costain was not at first afraid of her. Also, of course, all those we have questioned would have been thinking in terms of men.' His shoulders eased and he smiled momentarily. 'Thank you, Runcorn. I am obliged for your expert opinion, and of course for your time.'

Runcorn was unsatisfied. He had raised questions to Faraday; he had not given answers. How much was he seeing of the woman Olivia Costain had been, and how much was his picture of her coloured by Kelsall's feelings for her? How much was his feeling for Melisande? He was not doing his job. He had in the far distant past criticised Monk for emotions, usually impatience and anger. He was guilty of that now himself. How Monk would despise him!

And then with surprise, a lurch into freedom, he realised that he did not care. He could be hurt by other people's opinions of him, but he could no longer be twisted or destroyed by them.

He could learn more of Olivia Costain's life from others less close to her, seeing her with clearer eyes. And in doing that, he would also, discreetly, learn a great deal more about Alan Faraday. If there really were a violent and terrible envy, it could as easily be over him. And that might even mean that Melisande was in danger too.

Should he warn her? Of what? He had no idea.

Then even as he walked up the steep, winding road towards

the house where he hoped for a more dispassionate opinion of Olivia Costain, he realised that he did not believe the killer was a woman jealous of Olivia so much as possibly afraid of her. She challenged the order of things that they had to obey. She was disruption in the midst of certainty, the old ways mocked and the rules broken.

But who cared about that enough to kill the trespasser, the blasphemer? That could be a woman, or a man with his power, his authority, vested in the rules that do not change. He could even feel himself justified in getting rid of her before she destroyed even more.

The vicar, Costain? The chief constable, Faraday? Or Newbridge, the lord of the manor, with roots centuries deep in the land?

Runcorn came to the house and knocked. The woman who answered was white-haired and bent nearly double over her cane, but her eyes were unclouded and she had no difficulty hearing him when he spoke.

'Miss Mendlicott?'

'Yes I am. And who are you, young man? You sound like a Londoner to me. If you're lost, no use asking me the way. All the roads are new since I went anywhere.'

'I'm not lost, Miss Mendlicott,' Runcorn replied. 'It is you I would like to speak to. And you are right, I am from London. I'm in the police there, but it is about the death of Miss Costain I want to ask you. You taught her in school, didn't you?'

'Of course I did. I taught them all. But if I knew who had killed her, you wouldn't have had to come looking for me, young man. I've had sent for you. Don't keep me standing here in the cold. What's your name? I can't go on calling you "young man".' She squinted up at him. 'Not that you're so young, are you!'

'Superintendent Runcorn, Miss Mendlicott. And thank you, I would like to come in.' He did not tell her he was fifty. That made him twenty years older than Melisande.

She led him into a small sitting room with barely space for two chairs, but pleasantly warm. On the mantelshelf there was a small jug with fresh primroses and a spray of rosemary. Anglesey was always surprising him.

He told her without evasion that he was wishing to learn more of the men who had courted Olivia, and whom she had refused.

'Poor child,' the old lady said sadly. 'Understood everything, and nothing. Could name most of the birds in the sky when she was fourteen, and had no idea how few other people even looked at them. Blind as a bat, she was.'

Runcorn struggled to keep up with her. 'You mean she was naïve?'

'I mean she couldn't see where she was going!' Miss Mendlicott snapped. 'Of course she was naïve. Nothing wrong with her eyesight. Didn't want to look.'

'Did Sir Alan Faraday court her seriously, do you know?'

'Handsome boy,' she said, staring beyond him into the

winter garden with its bare trees. 'Good at cricket, as I recall. Or so someone told me. Never watched it myself. Couldn't make head nor tail of it.'

'Did he court Miss Costain?' he repeated.

'Of course he did. But she had no patience with him. Nice man, but tedious. She used to tell me about him. Came to see me every week. Brought me jam.' Her eyes filled with tears and she let them slide down her cheeks unashamed.

'She talked about Sir Alan to you?'

'Done well for himself,' she said, shaking her head a little. 'Grew up here, then went south to the mainland.'

'England?'

She gave him a withering look. 'Wales, boy! Wales!'

He smiled in spite of himself. 'But Olivia refused him.'

'Course she did. Liked him well enough. Kind man, when you get to know him, she said. Good horseman, patient, light hands. Need that on a horse. Heavy hands ruin a horse's mouth. Loves the land. Best thing about him,' she said.

'But she refused his offer of marriage?' He did not want to see Faraday as part of this wide, beautiful land with its wind and its endless distance, belonging to it, when Runcorn himself had to leave it and go back to the clatter and smoke of London. But he did want to think that there was a better side to him, a man who could love and give of himself, who could be gentle, handle power with a light touch.

'Was he angry that she refused him?' he persisted.

Miss Mendlicott looked at him as if he were a wilfully

95

obtuse student. 'Of course he was. Wouldn't you be? You offer a beautiful and penniless young woman your name and your place in society, your wealth and your loyalty, and she says she does not wish for it!'

Runcorn tried to imagine the scene. Had Faraday loved her? He certainly had not shown it when he spoke of her after her death. Had he forgotten her in his new love for Melisande? That was too raw in his mind to touch. 'Why did she refuse him? Was there someone else she preferred?'

Miss Mendlicott smiled. 'Not in any practical way. Sometimes she had very little sense. She could see the flowers in front of her, count their petals; and she could see the stars, and tell you their names. But she was fuzzy about the middle distance, as if there were mist over the field.' There were tears in her eyes again and she did not brush them away. She was not going to dissemble or excuse herself to a man from London – probably not to anyone else either.

'There was someone impractical,' he concluded. Had that been Kelsall after all, a young man who could still barely afford to keep himself, let alone a wife?

'A poet,' she replied. 'And explorer.' She snorted. 'Of all the romantic and ridiculous things to be. Off to the Mountains of the Moon, he was.'

'What?' Runcorn was jolted out of courtesy by shock.

'Africa!' the old lady said witheringly. 'Some of these explorers have very fanciful minds. Heaven knows where they would have ended up if she had gone with him.'

'She wanted to?' It was surprisingly painful to ask, because he could imagine the loneliness of being left behind. He had always been a practical man; the whole notion of dreams was new to him. He had reconciled himself to a solitary life. His friendships and his time and effort were absorbed in his increasingly demanding work. Now he was torn apart by impossible dreams. How could he criticise Olivia or fail to understand her?

The old lady was watching him with sharp, amused eyes. The age difference between them was sufficient that she could have taught him as a schoolboy, and that might well be how she was regarding him now.

'She did not confide in me,' she addressed his question. He knew it was her way of avoiding answering. And that meant that Olivia had loved the man as well as the adventure, but many things had made it impossible. Perhaps she had not even been asked.

How could the reality of Faraday, kind, honest but predictable, have matched the dream? It did not matter now, because Olivia had not gone, and she had refused Faraday, Newbridge and John Barclay, and no doubt worn out her long-suffering brother.

Runcorn thanked Miss Mendlicott and left.

He went back to the vicarage and disturbed Costain preparing the next Sunday's sermon. He looked tired and grieved, more as if he were searching for some thread of hope for himself than for others.

Runcorn felt a pang of compunction about disturbing him with what had to be painful, but such awareness had never hindered him before, and he could not allow it to now. There was a kind of comfort in duty.

'I don't know what further I can tell you,' Costain said wearily. 'Olivia could be exasperating, heaven knows, but I cannot imagine anyone being driven to such a rage as to do that to her. It was somebody quite mad. I just cannot think that anyone we know is so depraved.'

'Such things are always hard to understand,' Runcorn agreed. 'But it is inescapable that someone did.' He had no time to spare on retreading old ground, and no words that would change or heal anything. 'I believe there was a young poet and explorer she was fond of,' he said.

Costain frowned. 'Percival? Interesting man, and knowledgeable, but hardly a suitor for Olivia. He spoke well. But that was two years ago at least. And he went to Africa, or maybe it was South America. I don't recall.'

'Mountains of the Moon,' Runcorn supplied.

'I beg your pardon?' Costain's voice was sharp, as if he suspected Runcorn of a highly insensitive flippancy.

'In Africa.' Runcorn blushed. It was just the kind of clumsiness Monk accused him of. 'At least that is what I heard. Could such adventure have caught Miss Costain's imagination and perhaps made her compare more realistic suitors with something unattainable?'

'Probably!' Costain ran his hands over his brow, pushing

his hair back. 'Perhaps. But what does that have to do with her death? They grew impatient with her. Faraday is now going to marry Mrs Ewart, so I understand. Newbridge was annoyed because Olivia turned him down, but that is hardly a reason to lose his sanity altogether. He is a perfectly decent man. I've known him most of his life. His family have lived here for generations. He could find any number of other suitable young women. If you'll forgive me saying so, Mr Runcorn, you are looking for violent passion where there is only irritation and inconvenience, at the very worst disappointment. I cannot help but think you are looking in the wrong places.'

Runcorn had a deep fear that Costain was right. He was drawn to the emotions around Olivia and her betrothal, or lack of it, because he felt that was where the seat of much violence lay. Perhaps he saw so much in it just because he had fallen in love for the only time in his life.

But nothing would make him kill anyone over it, least of all Melisande. He wanted her happiness, he wished her to be loved and to marry a man worthy of her, which he could not see in Faraday. But then perhaps he would not see it in anyone?

He thanked Costain and asked to see his wife. With deep reluctance, permission was granted and Runcorn found himself in the sitting room opposite Naomi.

'Are you any closer to the truth, Mr Runcorn?' she asked almost as soon as the door was closed. She spoke very quietly, as if she did not wish her husband to overhear either her questions, or possibly Runcorn's answers.

'I am not sure,' he replied honestly. 'Miss Costain was not afraid of whoever killed her until the very last moment, when it was too late. That suggests it was someone she knew, possibly even cared for. And it was a crime of great violence, so profound emotion was involved.' He watched her face and saw the pain in it so deep guilt twisted inside him for causing it, and he knew how many times he must have done the same thing in the past, to others, and been less aware.

'You are saying it was someone who knew her well, and hated her.' Naomi stared out at the bare, winter garden and the tangled branches of the trees outlined against the sky. 'She did awaken strange feelings in other people, sometimes unease or a sense of loss for the unreachable. She was not content to be ordinary, but is that a sin?' She turned now to look at him, searching his eyes for a response. 'She reminded us of the possibilities we have not the courage to strive for. We are too afraid of failure. Does one kill for that?'

'One can kill for safety,' Runcorn answered, surprised at his own words. 'Did she threaten someone's comfort, Mrs Costain?'

She walked to the further side of the window. 'Not at all. It was a foolish thing to have said. I'm sorry. I don't even know what she was doing outside at that hour on a winter night. She must have quarreled with someone.'

'Over what?' he asked. 'Who would she meet in the church-yard? He came with a knife, as if he intended harm.'

She winced and shivered, holding her arms around herself. 'I have no idea.'

He had a sharp sense that she was lying. It was nothing obvious – the tightness in her shoulders, an altered tone in her voice. Was she protecting her husband? Or even herself? Was the threat that Olivia posed far closer to home than anyone had previously thought? Had Olivia, in desperation, tried to force her brother into keeping her for the rest of his life, and he had found the endless, draining expense too much to endure? Had his tortured self-control broken, and he had seized a terrible escape? It answered all they knew, every fact.

But what secret had cost Olivia her life? What did this quiet, sad, very conventional house hide?

'I think you have an idea, Mrs Costain,' he told her. 'You knew your sister-in-law as well as anyone did. You cared for her, and you understood her. You also must know the expense of her remaining unmarried, and refusing offer after offer for no reason she was prepared to give, unless it was to you?'

She turned to stare at him, anger flaring in her eyes, her mouth hard. 'If I knew who murdered Olivia, I would tell you. I do not. Nor do I know anything that would be of use to you. I have admitted that she was a disturbing person, and hard for many to understand. I can tell you nothing new. Please do not waste any more of your time, or mine, in asking me such things. Good day, Mr Runcorn. The maid will show you out.'

'How dare you behave with such crass insensitivity?' Faraday accused Runcorn that evening when he answered his summons to the big house. They were standing in the library. Now the gaslamps were lit and a good fire roared and hissed in the grate.

'You will not approach Mrs Costain on the subject again,' Faraday went on. 'If anything should be necessary to ask, I will do it. Have you no imagination at all how the poor woman must be feeling?' His face was red and his features pinched with anxiety and perhaps a sense of panic as failure crept closer around him. They knew nothing more than they had done the morning after Olivia was found. Every thread they pulled came loose in their hands. This was not Runcorn's jurisdiction; no one was going to blame him if Olivia's murder went unsolved. They expected nothing of him anyway.

'She is lying,' he said aloud. 'She knows something that could have provoked the kind of rage we saw in that murder.'

'Dear God!' Faraday exploded. 'Tell me you didn't say so to her!' He closed his eyes. 'You did! Don't bother to deny it, it's in your face. You oaf!' Suddenly he was shouting, his voice raw. 'This may be the way it is done in the alleys and brothels you usually police, but these are decent people, gentry, people of decency and some Christian values. Runcorn, the man's a vicar! Have you really no . . . ?' He drew in his breath and let out a heavy sigh. 'No. I suppose you haven't. It was my failure that I even let you in at the door.'

Runcorn felt as if the fire had burned out of the grate to scorch him. He was clumsy, and had always lacked the grace of someone gifted like Monk. He had achieved his rank by plodding patience, determination, the will to succeed, and perhaps now and then a flash of understanding of how the poor and the frightened had found ways of retaliating. He kept his word, so people trusted him, but he was not a gentleman; he had never known how to be.

'I did not tell her she lied,' he said quictly. 'I said I believed she knew something relevant that she had not said. She is complaining so hard because that is true.'

'Don't make it any worse!' Faraday begged. 'Man, you are like a cart horse in the dining room. Just get out of it! God alone knows who killed Olivia Costain, but we aren't going to find out your way.' His voice was rough with the edge of defeat. He must be hot, standing in this room so close to the fire, wearing his beautifully tailored jacket. It would be the best tweed, and cut with the casual elegance of one who does not need to impress.

And yet he did need to. The whole island was watching him, waiting for him to take away the burden of fear and tell them it was over, and justice would be done. And he had no idea how to do it – that was clear to Runcorn, even if not yet to anyone else.

To his chagrin, Runcorn was sorry for him. Not much was

expected of ordinary men. There was room for failure. It cost, but it was a familiar part of life. In men of Faraday's privilege and office, it was crippling. He would not know how to deal with it. Nothing had prepared him for the bitterness or the shame of defeat. Perhaps all his life he had been expected to fill a certain mould, to win, to take pain or loss without complaint.

Did he imagine that Melisande needed him to be faultless or she would not love him? Was that some legacy from his love of Olivia, or was it woven into his life and upbringing, inherited from his father, and his father before him? Did he think that if someone close to him, like a wife, were to know his weaknesses as well as his strengths, then they would use them to some kind of advantage, manipulate him, or mock him?

No one can be always right. Every man has his flaws, the places where he is desperately vulnerable. Never to attempt anything that may cause pain or defeat is to be a coward at life. One loves those brave enough to try. Runcorn had seen women at times love the defeated far more tenderly, more passionately than the victim. To love is to protect, to nurture, to need, and in turn be needed.

How did he know that, and Faraday did not?

The silence had lengthened and Runcorn had not yet even tried to defend himself. 'Then you had better look into the Costains yourself, sir,' he said eventually. 'Because there is much that she knows, but will not tell me.'

'Nonsense,' Faraday replied. 'Thank you for your help, but it is not proving of any use. You are free to leave Anglesey whenever you wish. Good day.'

Runcorn was beyond the gates of the drive and into the road when Melisande caught up with him.

'Mr Runcorn!'

He turned. They were level with the hedge now and hidden from the windows of the house. Maybe he would not see her many times more, certainly not alone. He stopped and faced her, looking at her, trying to imprint on his mind every line of her brow, cheek, lips, the colour and light of her eyes, so he would never forget.

'I heard Alan tell you to go,' she said anxiously. 'He does not realise how his voice carries. Please don't listen to him. He is frightened that none of us will solve this murder, and he will be blamed for that. He takes his responsibility very hard.'

'He doesn't wish me to stay,' Runcorn pointed out.

'Does that matter?' she asked. 'He needs you to; we all do. Someone killed Olivia and we cannot turn away from that as if it had been done by some force of nature, and not one of us. We will suspect each other until we know.'

'Do you know anything about the explorer she met about two years ago?' he asked. 'Could she have loved him?'

Melisande thought about it for several moments. 'She never said anything to me, but then why should she? We spoke often. I liked her right from the first time we met, but we talked more of books, ideas, places, far more than of people we knew, and never of men.'

Another darker thought occurred to Runcorn, but he could not mention anything so indelicate to Melisande, much less suggest it of a woman who had been her friend. He felt the heat on his skin even as he pushed the idea from his mind, although he could not dismiss it altogether.

'Do you think it is something to do with Mr Costain?' Melisande asked. 'Is that why you spoke to Naomi so bluntly?' She was trying to read the answer in his face, perhaps judge from it what he was unprepared to say.

'I think Mrs Costain may be trying to protect both her husband and Olivia,' Runcorn replied, guiding a path between truth and an outright lie. If Olivia were one of those rare women who prefer their own sex to the other, then it was an excellent reason why she would not wish to marry, and at the same time, it would be impossible for her to admit to it to anyone.

But what if someone had learned? Any man might feel unbearably betrayed to be rejected for another woman. It would be seen as the final insult to all that he believed of himself. It would be unendurable if anyone else found out. Was that what the quarrel with John had been about?

'Oh,' Melisande said softly. 'You do not need to be so delicate with me. I am aware of such things, in women as well as in men. But I had no sense that it was so with her.'

Now the blood scorched up Runcorn's face and he felt

ridiculous. If Faraday, not to mention Barclay, knew that he had even entertained such a thought in Melisande's presence, let alone discussed it with her, he would be appalled.

She was smiling, a flicker of real amusement in her eyes. 'I liked Olivia,' she told him. 'I felt comfortable with her, and very free to be honest, perhaps not only with her but with myself. And that is not always true for me. If I can bear the way she died, and think of the brutality, and the passion that caused it, then surely I can look at a little human frailty without turning away with thought only for myself? She deserved better than that of me. Moral queasiness is rather a cheap escape, don't you think?'

He looked at her, and for a moment the pity and the honesty in her face made her infinitely beautiful to him. Faraday, with his lumbering imagination and his simplistic judgements, was a clod, bitterly unworthy of her.

Did she know that he had once courted Olivia also? Should he tell her? Was it just a grubby and horribly obvious attempt to spoil her happiness because he envied any man who could spend time in her company, let alone marry her? Or was it the only real honesty, because Faraday might be involved in Olivia's death?

He had no idea. The only answer would be to learn more about Faraday and then judge what to say. It must be the truth, and it must be fair. It was Melisande who mattered, not whether she liked Runcorn for what he did, and certainly not whether Faraday liked him or not.

His face was still hot. He tried to smile back at her. 'I
don't like finding weaknesses in people, even if they help to
solve a crime, but I can't afford to ignore them or lie to
myself that they aren't there. I would like to have protected
you from having to think of it.'

'Thank you, Mr Runcorn,' she acknowledged. 'I do not
wish to be protected from life. I think we might miss a great
deal more of the good, and the bad would find us anyway.
At least the sense of emptiness would. I think I would rather
eat something unpleasant now and then, than perish of star-
vation sitting at the table because I was afraid to try. Please
find out what really happened to Olivia.'

She turned and walked away before he could find the words
to answer her, and repeat his promise.

He had no choice now but to look more deeply into Faraday's
life and character. He began where Miss Mendlicott had ended
and, through conventional methods, was able to look up his
days in Cambridge University where he was moderately
successful in gaining a degree in history, but he did not need
to earn his living by using it. He had travelled in Europe on
and off for a year or two in all the expected places before
joining the army. He did not see Venice or Capri. He did not
venture as far as Athens, which Runcorn had read about, and
would have leaped at the chance to see. He did not see the
beautiful city of Barcelona, named after Hannibal Barca, who
had crossed the Alps with elephants, to attack Rome, before

the days of Julius Caesar. That was one history lesson from schooldays that had fired Runcorn's imagination and he had never forgotten it.

Runcorn left the library in Bangor and walked out into the wind off the sea with his mind in a whirl. He had visited a different world where all the privileges he saw with class and money did not buy the magic he had assumed. If Faraday had dreams at all, they were not of legendary places of beauty, and the ghosts of the past. They seemed to be of the good opinions of others, perhaps domestic certainty and investment in the next generation of all that he had been bequeathed by his forebears.

As he walked down to the railway station Runcorn felt a sad, strange closeness to him. Faraday was in his early forties, and yet he wanted only safety, peace, and things to remain as they were.

Runcorn took the train to Caernarfon and continued his enquiries. He knew from long experience how to be discreet, to ask one thing while appearing to ask another. All he learned about Faraday confirmed the opinion that he was a decent man, but pedestrian, a man of likes and dislikes rather than of passions.

But Runcorn remembered with a jolt that that was what Monk had said of him: half-hearted, lacking the fire or the courage to grasp for more than he could safely reach, a man who never dared the boundaries or stepped into the unknown, as his bridges crumbled behind him. And Monk had despised him for it.

Did he now despise Faraday? Oddly, he did not. He pitied him and felt as if he were looking into a distorted mirror. There was something of himself in the man he saw, a man imprisoned in the expectations of others, too afraid of being disliked to follow his own vision, not hungry enough.

Did it take the face of one woman to stir you deeply enough to abandon comfort and follow impossible dreams into the cold infinity? Then why was Faraday half-heartedly in love with Melisande, not absurdly and hopelessly as Runcorn was?

The following day he stayed in Beaumaris and asked more questions, seemingly idling his time with local gossip and trivial pieces of information about the past.

In pretending to look for property to buy he invented a brother who had done well in trade. In this way he learned more of Newbridge, since his house was within sight of one place he viewed, across a stretch of sloping valley.

'Can't see it so well in the summertime,' the young man said who was accompanying him.

'Yes. I see what you mean,' Runcorn agreed. 'Looks like quite a decent place. Might that be for sale, Mr Jenkins?'

'Oh, no, sir. That belongs to Mr Newbridge. Been in his family for years.'

'Big family, has he?' Runcorn asked innocently. 'Good place for children, I imagine.'

'No, not married yet,' Jenkins replied.

'Betrothed, then?'

'Not as I know.' Jenkins was keen for a sale. 'Courting the vicar's sister, the poor young lady that was killed.'

Runcorn looked sceptical. 'Do you think Mr Newbridge might sell, if the offer were good enough?'

'No, sir, I don't. Money isn't everything.'

'Looks like a lot of land for one man to handle, and in none too good repair.' Runcorn squinted across the valley, the wind in his face. 'Cause resentment, will it, if an outsider buys old land?'

'Yes, sir, it could,' Jenkins said candidly. 'Newbridges've been here since the Civil War. Big thing to keep up, a position like this, being the last in the male line of the family, an' all, but he'll soon find the right wife, and then there'll be sons to carry on.'

Runcorn was struck with a sudden horror at the weight of such responsibility, the need to marry, the burden of expectation. Too many people cared what he did, were watching and needing him to produce sons and fill the needs of the future.

Was some of that why he responded badly to Barclay, and why he had taken Olivia's rejection with anger as well as disappointment. Had she said something about him that might make it even harder for him to find a wife who was willing and able to take up this responsibility that was so enormous to him? Newbridge had no title, no hereditary office, not even great wealth, just a family name and lands he was tied to by history. Was he always trying to keep up with other

111

men he felt had more to give, more charm, more heritage, more hope of office in the future?

It would make him an easy mark for Barclay's cruelty.

'I think I'll wait until I've been in touch with my brother, thank you,' Runcorn said to Jenkins. 'I'll let you know.'

Faraday sent for Runcorn that evening. He looked tired and disappointed, and even though he had demanded Runcorn's presence he paced the carpet in front of the fire and seemed reluctant to broach the subject.

They spoke of trivia. Outside the rain lashed at the windows and the wind was rising steadily, roaring in off the great sweep of the Atlantic.

Runcorn grew impatient. 'If you've learned something, sir, and I can be of help, perhaps you'd tell me what it is.'

Faraday winced at Runcorn's lack of polish, and instantly Runcorn felt gauche. He had a hideous vision of his doing something appalling that he did not even understand until too late, and Melisande being ashamed of him. Except that that was absurd. She might be disgusted. To be ashamed one had to care, to feel some kind of kinship with the one at fault.

Faraday was still pacing back and forth, lost in his own inabilities.

'You suggested that Miss Costain might have discovered something about her own family, a secret that was shameful or embarrassing,' he began. 'And that she threatened to expose it if her brother did not give her more freedom.'

112

Runcorn was unhappy but the ugliness of the thought did not invalidate it. He was afraid that it could be true, and Naomi's strong, weary face filled his mind. 'I thought of it as unlikely but not impossible,' he conceded.

Faraday's voice was heavy. 'I'm grateful for your professional skill, and glad I don't have to share the kind of experience that has given it to you.'

In spite of the fire, Runcorn felt colder.

'You recognised a crime committed with intense hatred,' Faraday continued. 'I used to assume all murders were, but you exposed the difference for me to see. I should be obliged to you for that also, but I'm not sure that I am.'

'Do you know something further?' Runcorn demanded, his voice betraying his emotion. 'You didn't send for me in this weather to thank me for teaching you a part of your job you'll almost certainly never need again.'

A slow stain of colour spread up Faraday's cheeks. 'Yes I do, but I have more yet to learn. Mrs Costain is concealing something of which she is deeply ashamed, or if not ashamed, then at least terrified that it might become known. Costain's sister was slaughtered like an animal. Now it looks as if his wife might be an adulteress and have conceived to another man the child she never bore him.' His voice choked with emotion, and for a moment he was unable to speak. His strong hands clenched at his sides until the knuckles shone white, and he could not keep them still.

Runcorn felt the wave of misery engulf him also. Had it

been Olivia's own need for freedom that had driven her to confront Naomi, or the defence of her brother? Murder is never without pain, but this seemed even more steeped in it than most. He would rather not have known, but he was not a coward, at least not from the realities of his job. At this moment his own frailties were irrelevant.

Faraday was staring at him still.

'What is it?' Runcorn demanded.

Faraday's voice was little more than a whisper, all but choking off at the end. 'The baby is dead. It looks as if she killed him.'

Runcorn was stunned, as if he had walked face first into a wall and the pain of it dizzied his senses. Naomi Costain with her strange, powerful face, and a late born, illegitimate child, which she had murdered with her own hands. Why? To hide her adultery? The obvious thought. But perhaps the child had been misshapen, abnormal? He found himself blinking and his throat inexplicably tight and rough. Could that be forgiven, such a helpless child robbed of life? Or snatched from pain? Or was she only saving herself, her humiliation? And then to be faced with blackmail by Olivia?

'I can't do anything,' he said. 'You'll need police authority to follow that.' It was not cowardice speaking, though he was glad he had no jurisdiction here.

'I'll get it for you,' Faraday said hoarsely. 'Please, Runcorn? These people are my friends, my neighbours. I have no idea how to deal with a crime like this.'

It was on the edge of Runcorn's tongue to remind Faraday

that it was he who had discovered this element of tragedy while Runcorn had not even guessed at it. Olivia, possibly, but not Naomi! He had talked with Naomi and seen nothing of this in her, no unfed hunger that consumed all honour and loyalty, no loss of her only child, to whatever brutal end. His professional skills that he had relied on so heavily to define who he was had failed him completely.

It was Faraday, whose profound judgement he despised, who had seen the answer. Faraday, who was going to marry Melisande.

He should be grateful, for her sake, that he was not the fool that Runcorn had thought him. That should comfort him as he walked away down the hill, wind harder and traces of snow making a flurry of white in the gloom.

Runcorn turned over and over in his mind during the night everything he had learned, and the sense of his own failure deepened. He had come to Anglesey as a stranger. He loved this vast silence disturbed only by the wind and the echo of waves on the shore. People here spoke more slowly, and there was a lilt of music in their voices, but he knew now that he only imagined he understood them. He had been as wrong as possible, not only about Olivia, who had stooped to blackmailing her own family, and Naomi whom he had believed so strong, but who had betrayed her husband, then her child, and finally Olivia. The one skill he believed he possessed had left him.

How did Faraday know about the blackmail? Had Naomi admitted anything? Runcorn would not leave it like this, so many questions unanswered, so many of his own impressions mistaken.

As soon as he had dressed and had breakfast, he walked across the crisp frost and the pale fingers of new snow whitening the windward sides of the uneven ground. Far in the distance Snowdonia gleamed white.

He was admitted to the vicarage straight away, and Naomi came to the morning room where he had been asked to wait. He rose to his feet as she closed the door behind her and invited him to be seated again.

'Good morning, Mr Runcorn,' she said gravely.

He struggled to take all emotion from his face, even his voice. He was unnaturally stiff, but he could not help it. Defeat and an overwhelming sense of loneliness almost choked him.

'Good morning, Mrs Costain.' What could he say to her that was not absurd? Obviously Faraday had not spoken to her yet. She was almost at the end, and she had no idea. Within months she could be hanged. This was a nightmare in which reality itself was not safe.

'What can I do for you? There is nothing further I can tell you.' Her face was bland, polite, not exactly at peace, but less scoured with grief than before, as if she were beginning to make terms with it. Was she denying to herself what she had done, or merely a superb actress?

116

'Miss Costain had three suitors that I knew of, ma'am: Mr Faraday some time ago, then Mr Newbridge, and most recently Mr Barclay. She declined them all. Did you favour any of those for her?'

'No,' Naomi said easily. 'I had no desire that she should marry without love. Mere affection would never have been enough for Olivia. She would have been wretched with a good but tepid man like Alan Faraday. It would have made them both unhappy, because he would have been aware of his failure to please her and it would have both confused and hurt him. She was not wise enough to know how to hide it. Melisande Ewart is gentler, much older within herself. She will probably accept the inevitable and if she has tears of despair, she will hide them from him. She is also, I think, kinder than Olivia. She will bring out the best in Alan, and he will never know it was she who did it, nor will she ever say so.'

Runcorn was overtaken with a sense of loss almost like a physical darkness, as if he were exiled far from all light and fire and the sound of laughter. He was too numb even to answer her.

'Newbridge is a good man, so far as I know,' she went on gravely, almost as if she were speaking as much to herself as to him. 'But I cannot say that I like him. My husband chides now for it, but regardless, I had no wish that Olivia should marry him if she did not wish to. He wants many children in order to establish his family again. I am not sure

Olivia wished to be that kind of woman. If you are devoted to a man then it is a pleasure, and a privilege to work beside him, but if you are not it is an imprisonment, a lifelong denial of yourself.'

In his mind's eye he saw the woman who had walked past him in green, her head high, and he was glad she had escaped. Then he realised what he was saying, and who had brought him to that vision, and he was disgusted with himself. What had happened to the instincts he used to have?

'And as for John Barclay,' Naomi went on, 'Olivia did not refuse him, it was he who rejected her, suddenly and very bluntly.' Now there was pain in her voice, but not the anger Runcorn would have expected. It was like an old wound reopened, not the outrage of a new one. Again he had the certainty that there was something profound about Olivia that this woman was hiding from him, perhaps from everyone.

'Did she know Mr Barclay before this recent courtship?' he asked, the question suddenly urgent.

Now the anger was there in her eyes, blazing up for an instant. 'No,' she said without hesitation. 'Why do you ask?'

'It seems . . . brutal, if she did not rebuff him.'

'It was,' she agreed with a twist of her mouth. 'But I do not think John Barclay is a nice man. He did not love Olivia, he wanted her, as a collector wants a rare and beautiful butterfly, to preserve it, not for its happiness. He will be content to put a pin through its body and capture its colours for ever in death.'

Runcorn remembered Olivia's body on the graveside, stained with blood, and thought for a moment that he was going to be sick.

'I'm sorry,' Naomi said very quietly. 'That was a bad thing for me to say. I apologise for it. Perhaps my grief is not as well-controlled as I imagined. Please forgive me.'

Faraday was wrong, he had to be. There was a further answer to find. Perhaps he too was trying to protect Melisande from the fact that her brother was a cruel and manipulative man. But Runcorn knew that it could not be done. No matter how much you love, covering evil and allowing the innocent to walk in the shadow of blame was not a path he could take. There is no light at the end of it.

'Thank you, Mrs Costain,' he said gently. 'Anger is like a knife: it can be dangerous out of control, but you need it sometimes, to cut away what needs to go.'

Her eyes widened with a flare of surprise. 'Are you still working on the case, Mr Runcorn? I thought you had given up. I'm so glad I was mistaken.' The shadow was still there across her face; the lie she clung on to came in the midst of the other honesty.

'Yes. I'm still working,' he said, knowing that that, at least, was true.

Disliking every step of it, Runcorn traced Barclay's actions over the last days before Olivia's death. Discretion was a skill he had learned over his professional life. It was not difficult to discover that Barclay had shown a great curiosity about Olivia. He was courting her, in rivalry with Newbridge; it was natural he should seek to know all he could about her.

Then it grew clearer that it was actually Naomi whose actions he was following, she in whose travels, whose expenditure he showed such an interest.

Runcorn's mind whirled. What had Barclay been seeking? He had come here asking questions about Naomi, looking for times and dates, patterns of behaviour? He had visited a hotel, a hospital, a church, a quiet doctor with a small, expensive practice. Runcorn went to see the doctor, inventing an excuse, and found a handsome man in his fifties, courteous and distinctly uncommunicative.

Was it possible Faraday was right after all? An illegitimate child fitted all these facts and places. In the later stages Olivia had come with her.

Why had she come? Had Naomi been desperate, perhaps heavy with child and in need of help? She had trusted the one person on earth she should not have.

Except how could her husband not have known? Were they so distant that that was possible? What ice was in that house, or what storms, in those days?

That was some time after Olivia had sought refuge in friendship with the explorer poet, and longed to go with him to Africa, or wherever it was he intended. Had she remained at home because it was impossible for a woman to go to such parts of the world? Or had he simply not asked her? Or was it from duty to look after her sister-in-law in terrible distress, and for the life of the child, if nothing else?

And then Naomi had killed the child anyway.

Runcorn wondered how he could have seen nothing of that in their faces. Or was he looking at the whole thing from the wrong side? The love story was Olivia's, not Naomi's. The child was Olivia's, and it was Naomi who had protected her, and was still protecting her name, even after she was dead.

What had happened to the child? Was it not a far greater sin to kill a live child than to abort one before it was born? Abortion was dangerous for the mother, but so was birth.

He turned and walked into the wind, to the doctor's house. A brass plate informed him the man's name was Medway. Runcorn knocked on the door, in spite of the late hour. If he missed the last train back from Bangor and spent the night on this side of the strait, it was immaterial.

'Yes, Mr Runcorn?' the doctor said curiously, when Runcorn had been shown in and announced.

Runcorn already knew what he meant to do. 'I have a story to tell you,' he said. 'And it is necessary that you listen to what I say. If you are not free to comment, I will understand, but you know the truth of what is being said, and you may decide that I need to know the truth of what happened.'

The doctor smiled. 'In that case you had better come in.'

Runcorn accepted swiftly, and over an excellent supper by the fire, he told Dr Medway of Olivia's death, what he had deduced and what was said only or hinted at darkly.

'I see,' Medway said finally, his voice carrying the weight of tragedy in it, overlaid with anger for the present. 'You understand I cannot betray confidences, Mr Runcorn?'

'Yes,' Runcorn agreed.

Medway's face was very pale. 'The child died soon after birth. It was one of the most harrowing losses of my experience. I fought all I could to save him, but it was beyond my skill, or I believe, anyone's. No one was to blame, least of all the mother.'

Runcorn pictured Olivia, weeping over the baby she had paid so much to bring into the world. Perhaps Percival had been the man whom she had truly loved. She had given up going with him in order to carry and deliver the child, and yet he had died. Or perhaps he had not been worthy of her, not loved her in return more than the swift infatuation of the moment. Runcorn chose to believe the former.

Thank God Naomi had been there, so at least she had not been alone. And she was even now protecting Olivia's memory, even if narrow and vicious men like John Barclay were happy to malign her.

Of course! That was why he had quarrelled with her and dramatically ceased to court her! Did he hate her for that? She had in a way deceived him, allowed him to believe she was fit for him to marry. Would she ever have told him? Or if he had not found out, might she have accepted him? No. But did he know that, or did his arrogance imagine she was intent on trapping him?

Had Newbridge known? Was that why he too had apparently lost interest in her? There was nothing to suggest he had suspected anything. Runcorn had found no trace of him in his pursuit of Naomi. If he had known, then could it be that Barclay had told him?

Why? He could have let Newbridge marry her, and told him afterwards. That would have been an exquisite revenge.

But upon whom? Newbridge! And it was Olivia who had deceived him. Runcorn had learned enough about the gentry to understand that if that had happened, Barclay himself might have suffered a certain ostracism. They would have closed ranks about Newbridge, here in Anglesey at least. Word would have spread. Faraday, soon to be Barclay's brother-in-law, would have believed it a betrayal.

However, if Barclay told Newbridge beforehand, that could be regarded as the act of a friend.

What would Melisande think of that? Runcorn was uncertain. To him it was an act of cruelty he found repellent, but then he had in his own mind seen so much of Melisande in Olivia, the same loneliness, the dreams that could never be realised, the hunger for something more than the daily obedience to the expectations of those who loved them, protected them, and imprisoned them with failure to understand.

Or perhaps it was he who did not really understand. He confused the romantic with the real.

And he was no closer to proving who had slashed Olivia with a carving knife in hatred for duping him, letting her

123

believe she was all he wanted, when he was nothing she wanted. Was that Barclay, or Newbridge? Runcorn was terribly afraid that it was Barclay, and the revelation of it would hurt Melisande unbearably. It might even prevent her marriage to Faraday, or anyone else that could make her happy, and safe.

What could Runcorn do to prove Barclay's innocence, that would not ruin Olivia's reputation and hurt irreparably the people who had loved her? And even showing Barclay innocent of murder could not conceal that his cruelty was self-serving and repellent.

He would start again with every detail about Barclay. It might be possible to prove that he could not have taken the knife from the kitchen and followed after Olivia up to the graveyard, or perhaps that he could not have returned and changed his clothes, disposed of them without anyone knowing. Maybe he could prove no clothes were missing. It would be long and tedious, but for Melisande's sake it would be done.

It took Runcorn two careful, unhappy days to ascertain that Barclay had learned enough of the story to be sure of the rest, and had certainly spoken alone with Newbridge just before Newbridge had been seen in such a rage as to be white-faced, and almost blind to those around him, two days before Olivia's death.

Runcorn felt gradually more sick with every new piece of

information. It looked as if Barclay could have killed Olivia, and was carefully making it appear that Newbridge had.

The evening of the second day he met with Faraday.

Faraday was angry and embarrassed, his face pink, not only from the warmth of the room, but in the high flush that comes from emotion.

'You've been investigating John Barclay,' he said as soon as Runcorn had closed the door. 'For God's sake, man, if you felt you had to do it, could you not at least have been a little more careful? I told you Mrs Costain knew some secret; I didn't expect you to tread exactly in Barclay's footsteps, and then all but imply he was incriminated in it! He'd never even been to Anglesey at that time! What on earth are you thinking of?'

Runcorn was startled. Had he really been so clumsy that Barclay already knew he was pursued? Apparently. Or were they the suspicions of a guilty man, always looking over his shoulder because he expected pursuit?

The only honest answer now was to tell Faraday what he had learned.

When he had finished Faraday stared at him, all the hectic colour drained from his face. 'Are you certain of this, Runcorn?' he asked.

'I'm certain of all I've told you,' Runcorn replied. 'I'm not yet sure what it means.'

'It means poor Olivia was killed for it,' Faraday said sharply.

Runcorn was still standing, cold and unhappy, blocked

from the fire by Faraday, perhaps unconsciously. 'Yes, but by Newbridge, or Barclay?'

'Find out,' Faraday commanded him. 'And for the love of heaven, this time be discreet.'

In the morning Runcorn left early to begin again. The ground rock hard from the frost and the grass edges were white. Even so, Melisande was waiting for him at the end of the road. He barely recognised her at first, she was so closely wrapped around with her cloak that it hid the outline of her body and shielded her face. She seemed to be staring towards the sea, until she heard his boots crunching the ice, then she turned.

'Good morning, Mr Runcorn.' Even in so few words her voice was sharpened with fear.

He felt the same twist of emotion inside himself, fiercer than before. He would have given anything he had to be able to protect her from this, but there was no bargaining with truth.

'Good morning, Mrs Ewart.' It would be absurd to ask her if she was waiting for him. There was no other reason she would be standing here growing steadily colder. He searched her eyes, wide and dark with dread.

She did not waste words. She was trembling with cold. 'Alan told me that he has discovered why John ceased to court Olivia. I believe he told you also.' That was barely a question, but the disappointment was painful, a dull ache beneath the words.

126

Temptation surged up inside him to tell her that it was he, not Faraday, who had found the truth, but he did not want to tell her until he had proven that it was not Barclay who had killed Olivia, but Newbridge. He drew in his breath to explain, and realised how intensely it was for his own sake. It was not she whose heart he longed to ease, but his own, because she thought he had let her down. He wished her to think well of him. Vanity, and above all, his own hunger.

That was why Faraday had taken the credit for something he had not done, because he needed Melisande to think him cleverer than he was.

Runcorn took a deep breath and swallowed it down. 'Yes,' he said simply. 'The child was hers. He died almost immediately, so she never needed to tell anyone else. And perhaps the loss was easier to bear if other people did not speak of it.'

Melisande's eyes swam with tears. She struggled to speak, and failed. Her pity for Olivia was so intense it drowned out even her fear for Barclay. For moments they stood there in the ice and the widening morning light, overshadowed by the same aching grief. The sun sparkled on frost, as if the rough grass were encrusted with diamonds. In the distance the sea was flat calm, its surface disturbed only by currents and little ruffles of breeze, like the weft of silk.

'I wish I had known,' Melisande said at length. 'I would at least have told her that it made no difference to my care for her. How terribly alone she must have been.'

127

'Not alone,' he said gently. 'Naomi was always with her.'

She turned to him, hope flaring up in her eyes. 'Was she? Please don't tell me something to comfort me if it is not true. Please, always tell me the truth. I need one person who doesn't lie, however kind the reason.'

'I won't lie,' he promised rashly. He would have promised her anything. 'Naomi never let her down.'

She smiled slowly, a soft sadness filling her face, more beautiful to him than the radiance of the sun over the ground. 'Thank you,' she said sincerely. 'I must go, before they ask me why my morning walk took so long. Please . . . please don't stop your search. It is too late now to hide anything.' And without waiting for his answer, she walked with increasing speed up the hill back towards the great house.

Runcorn began straight away. He loathed Barclay and he despised him for what he seemed to have done both to Olivia and to Newbridge, but still he wanted to prove beyond all further question that he was not legally guilty of murder even if morally he was, though that was a different issue and the law had no remedy for it.

Runcorn knew the date of the birth – it was a matter of tracing back to nine months before that. He was already convinced that Costain knew nothing about the child. His eagerness to marry Olivia to first Faraday, then Newbridge, and finally Barclay, meant that either he was unaware of her child, and his death, or he was unbelievably insensitive. Runcorn was certain it was the former.

Still, he should ask Naomi again.

She received him in her own room in the vicarage, a quiet space on the ground floor filled with gardening gloves and secateurs, string, outdoor boots and trugs for carrying cut blooms and greenery. She was arranging a bowl of holly with berries like blood, and sprigs of evergreen that he could not name. Other berries were dark red as wine, and the bowl also glowed with carefully placed purple onions and red and black winter fruit.

He admired it, quite honestly. There was a rich warmth to it, as if it proclaimed hope and abundance in a dark season.

He did not waste her time, or his own, with prevarication. 'Do you know who was the father of Olivia's child, Mrs Costain?'

'Yes,' she said simply. 'But it was no one you know, and I have no desire to harrow up his emotions or ruin his reputation, so there is no purpose in your pursuing it. He never knew she was with child, and he is too far away from here to have had any part in her death.'

'Percival, I assume,' he concluded. 'I had not thought it was Mr Newbridge, but I needed to be certain.'

'Newbridge?' She looked startled, almost amused. 'Good heavens, no! Whatever made you imagine that?'

'You are perfectly sure?' he persisted.

'Perfectly,' she said with feeling. 'But if you doubt me, you can prove it for yourself. He was away in England at the time – Wiltshire, I think. Certainly he was miles from here.

129

He was staying with his sister, and buying cattle, or something of the sort. At that time he was more concerned with improving his livestock than gaining a wife. He has considerable responsibility, but to tell the truth, I think he wears it hard.'

'What sort of man was Percival?' Another idea was gaining strength in Runcorn's mind.

She smiled, placing a last golden onion in its place to complete the light and shade of the arrangement.

'I never thought of using onions like that,' he said with admiration.

'One uses what one has,' she replied. 'And onions keep very well. What was Percival like? He was fun, full of ideas, an imagination which could make you laugh and cry at the same time. He was not particularly handsome, but his face was unique, and he had a smile which lit up his eyes and made you feel as if you could survive anything as long as he liked you.'

'And did he like Olivia?' He did not want to hear that he had not; he could imagine her pain too deep in his own heart. But if that was so, he had to know.

Naomi looked away. 'Oh, yes, as much as she loved him, I think. But he was young and poor, and full of dreams. It will be years before he can afford to marry, if ever. And he was not suitable for a girl of Olivia's breeding. My brother would look far higher than a penniless wanderer for her. My mother-in-law was a lady,' she added. 'Very little money, but a heritage back to Norman days.' She sighed. 'Which is slightly absurd since, if you think about it, we must all have a heritage back to Eve, or we would not be here. We simply cannot name them. I don't give a fig who my ancestors were, only what I am, because that I can do something about. Am I proud of them is of far less meaning than would they be proud of me?'

Runcorn stared at her.

She looked back levelly. 'Are you asking me if Olivia could or would have married him? She would have, but he had more sense than to ask her. Newbridge did, and she refused him. Kindly, I hope.'

There it was, as clear as it would ever be. Newbridge had offered her all he had, and she had refused him. And John Barclay had told him that she had been willing to lie with an explorer with neither land nor family, and to bear his illegitimate child. That must have been to him the ultimate insult, not only to his love but to all his lineage, his values and his manhood. It remained now only to trace his exact actions on the night of her death, perhaps even to find the knife, or prove from where it was missing, or the clothes he had worn, and probably destroyed.

That was something Faraday had the power to do. Runcorn thanked Naomi and left, out into a day so cold the air stung his skin and the breath of the wind was like ice between the folds of his scarf.

Faraday conducted the search and found the last pieces,

as Runcorn had suggested. The knife was hidden in one of the barns. It took some care, but traces of blood were found, and Trimby agreed that the blade matched the wounds. More incriminating than that, they found the ashes of the clothes Newbridge had worn that night. There was not sufficient left to identify them, but the suit was gone and Newbridge could not explain its absence. He might have considered claiming to have given it to someone, but there was no one to substantiate it. The truth was terribly and agonisingly clear.

Newbridge was arrested and taken to the police cells in Bangor. Faraday told the waiting journalists and the public, briefly and with dignity, that the case was over, and justice would be done. The truth would be told at trial in due course. For now, the solution was plain, and he spoke for Olivia's family and for all the people of Anglesey when he reminded them that tomorrow was Christmas Eve. He asked for respite so they might all, for a brief time, remember the season and give thanks for the birth and life of Christ, and the hope of forgiveness and renewal in the world.

Runcorn stood in the crowd and felt the surge of gratitude that some kind of resolution had been reached, and there was justice and healing ahead. The admiration for Faraday was palpable in the air, a new respect that was more than for the office: this was for the man himself, and the patience and skill he had shown. They believed in him. They would not forget this, please heaven, the most horrific case Anglesey would ever know.

Not once did Faraday mention Runcorn's name, let alone suggest that he had been the one to find the solution.

Runcorn separated himself from the crowd and walked away towards the wide sweep of the water. The sun, low in the west, was making the great span of the bridge look like black fretwork on the sky across the burning colours of the sunset-painted water.

He would leave now. Melisande was as safe as he could make her. Barclay was shallow and manipulative, a man of innate cruelty, but Faraday would protect her from the worst of that. It was the best he could hope for. At least now Faraday would not have to prove himself any more. There must be a certainty that he had succeeded and even Barclay would be held back from criticism. He could hardly do anything but give his blessing to the marriage.

The wind stung Runcorn's eyes and he blinked hard. He refused to acknowledge, even to himself, that they were tears. But he was smiling as well. It was he who had solved the case, he who had found justice for Olivia, and some kind of safety for Melisande. She would never know Faraday had not been as clean, or as humble, as he allowed people to suppose.

Runcorn was second fiddle, never first, but he had played the more beautiful tune, and that was something he had never done before. This great clean land and water, with its light, its horizon beyond dreaming, had made a better man of him. He did not need anyone else to reassure him of that. He would carry it away with him, a better gift for Christmas than all the wealth, the food, the colours or the rejoicing of bells.

'Mr Runcorn.'

He turned round slowly. Melisande was standing on the quay behind him, the wind in her hair and the sunset light on her face. He gulped, all his resolve blown away in a single instant's meeting her eyes.

'Thank you,' she said gently. Her cheeks were burning, more than the fire on the water could reflect. 'I know it was you who worked out who killed Olivia, and why. And I know my brother well enough to guess at the part he played. I long ago ceased to believe he was a nice person, but I am grateful that you tried to protect me from knowing the extent of his cruelty.'

Runcorn could still think of nothing to say. He wanted to tell her that he loved her, he would always love her, and no price to his own pride or ambition was too great to pay for her happiness. But that would only embarrass her, and forfeit the last, brief thread of friendship that they had, and that he could keep bound to his heart.

'You gave Alan all the pieces, didn't you?' she asked.

He would not answer. It was the last temptation, and he refused to succumb. He had only a moment's weakness when he even thought he might. He smiled at her. 'He's going to make a good policeman.'

'I hope so,' she agreed. 'I think it matters to him. But he is not as good as you are, because there will probably never be another case like this.' She took a deep breath and let it out slowly. 'And he is not as good a man as you are. Truth means less to him, and he does not seek it for its own sake.'

He felt his cheeks burn. He would never all his life forget this moment. From now on, for ever, he would strive to be the man she had said he was to her. He wanted to tell her how great a gift that was, that the fire of it burned inside him lighting every corner, every wish or thought, but there were no words big enough, gracious enough, articulate enough for him to tell her.

'Mr Runcorn,' she said impatiently, her face burning, 'do I have to ask you if you love me? That is so undignified for a woman.'

He was stunned. She knew. All his careful concealment, his efforts to behave with dignity had been for nothing.

'Yes,' he said awkwardly. 'Of course I do. But . . .'

'But you don't want a wife?'

'Yes! Yes, I do . . . but . . .'

He was paralysed. This was not possible.

She lowered her eyes and slowly turned away.

He took a step after her, and another, catching her arm gently, but refusing to let go. 'Yes, I do, but I could not marry anyone else. Every time I looked at her, I would wish she were you. I've never loved before, and I cannot again.'

She smiled at him. 'You don't need to, Mr Runcorn. Once will be enough. If you would be so good as to ask me, I shall accept.'